"Don't get too close to any one camper."

It was a casual remark, but Nate's tone didn't sound casual.

Hayley raised an eyebrow. "I'm not close to anyone yet. But that Jeremy, he tugs at my heart."

"You'll learn to keep your distance," Nate said. "As for Jeremy, he needs to toughen up."

"He needs emotional support." She frowned. "Just because he's a boy, that doesn't mean he's not allowed to have feelings."

"I *have* worked with a lot of young people." Nate sounded either defensive or patronizing.

Either way, it annoyed her. "So have I."

They were glaring at each other. Nate's eyes glittered in the firelight.

Wow, handsome. Stray, distracting thought. Their gazes tangled now in a different way.

"Okay, full disclosure." He looked away for a few seconds, then looked back, smiling a little. "I've never been in charge of a group of teens before."

"Nor have I," she admitted. "The first two days went pretty well, but I'm worried about how the rest of the camp session will go."

"We'll get through it together."

Lee Tobin McClain is the *New York Times* bestselling author of emotional small-town romances featuring flawed characters who find healing through friendship, faith and family. Lee grew up in Ohio and now lives in Western Pennsylvania, where she enjoys hiking with her goofy goldendoodle, visiting writer friends and admiring her daughter's mastery of the latest TikTok dances. Learn more about her books at www.leetobinmcclain.com.

Books by Lee Tobin McClain

Love Inspired

K-9 Companions

Her Easter Prayer
The Veteran's Holiday Home
A Friend to Trust

Rescue Haven

The Secret Christmas Child
Child on His Doorstep
Finding a Christmas Home

Redemption Ranch

The Soldier's Redemption
The Twins' Family Christmas
The Nanny's Secret Baby

Visit the Author Profile page at LoveInspired.com for more titles.

A Friend to Trust

Lee Tobin McClain

LOVE INSPIRED
INSPIRATIONAL ROMANCE

LOVE INSPIRED®
INSPIRATIONAL ROMANCE

Recycling programs
for this product may
not exist in your area.

ISBN-13: 978-1-335-58652-0

A Friend to Trust

Copyright © 2023 by Lee Tobin McClain

For questions and comments about the quality of this book, please contact us
at CustomerService@Harlequin.com.

Love Inspired
22 Adelaide St. West, 41st Floor
Toronto, Ontario M5H 4E3, Canada
www.LoveInspired.com

Printed in U.S.A.

There is therefore now no condemnation
to them which are in Christ Jesus, who walk
not after the flesh, but after the Spirit. For
the law of the Spirit of life in Christ Jesus
hath made me free from the law of sin and death.
—*Romans* 8:1–2

To Andrea, who suggested the perfect
finishing touch for my pastor hero.

Chapter One

"Mom! You said Mr. Stan would be in charge here."

The boy's anxiety-laced words made Hayley Harris look up from the paperwork she was frantically trying to complete on each new camper at the Bright Tomorrows Residential Academy's summer camp.

Standing above her at the outdoor check-in table was the ninth teen boy in the group of twenty-eight campers. All young teenagers, and all somehow at risk. The one in front of her appeared to be about thirteen, tall and lanky, and he was looking worriedly at his frowning mother.

Hayley pushed back her hair. Why hadn't she brought a ponytail holder? It was hot in the afternoon sunshine.

She took a deep breath, then another, and managed a sympathetic smile. *She* had expected Stan

Davidson to be in charge here, too. His absence meant she was winging it, getting all the campers registered while appearing to be a calm, confident leader.

That shouldn't be a problem. She'd run the school cafeteria for three years and was used to hectic situations. Stan knew her and her qualifications well, and he'd hired her for the camp position almost as soon as she'd applied.

But there was a lot riding on this job. If she hoped to get the recommendations she needed for her fast-track teacher-training program, she needed to shine as a camp co-director. Even if things weren't going according to plan. Even if Stan, her far more experienced partner, had gone AWOL.

The air smelled of the large ponderosa pines that surrounded the school grounds. Behind the mother-son pair, the Colorado Rocky Mountains loomed, gorgeous, still snowcapped even in mid-June. God had created the mountains, and the worried boy, and the Bright Tomorrows Academy where the camp was being held. He knew everything that was going to happen today, and He had it under control.

Calmed by the natural beauty and her understanding of where it came from, she felt her shoulders loosen. Everything would be okay.

Unfortunately, the environment wasn't having the same effect on the mother and son in front of her.

"The brochure indicated that Stan Davidson was in charge," the mother said to the boy then frowned at Hayley as if she'd outright lied or else kidnapped her co-director. "I spoke to him just yesterday, and he didn't mention a word about not being here."

Nothing was going as planned today, but Haley mustered up a smile. She *had* to make this work. Had to help these boys have breakthroughs this summer. To Hayley, it was personal. And this summer job was her big chance. "Stan is running behind today, but I'm sure he'll be here any minute. Meanwhile, your name?"

"He's Jeremy Ruffles, and he needs a male influence." The boy's mother stepped closer.

"He'll get plenty of that." Hayley tried to make eye contact with the boy and failed because he was staring down at his feet, chewing on his lower lip. Poor kid. She scanned the group of counselors standing near the dorm building behind her. There was Markus, a kind college-aged intern, and she beckoned to him. "Could you take Jeremy to room…" She checked her list. "To room 302, and help him get settled?" Using the residential school as a camp meant the boys got to stay in a dormitory, not tents or cabins.

"Sure thing. Come on this way."

Only as Jeremy and his mother turned and started walking away did Hayley see the dog beside the boy. A gorgeous, fluffy-white Samoyed, wearing a red vest that identified it as a working dog. The dog trotted beside Jeremy, bumping against his leg, so striking that people stopped their conversations to stare at it and smile.

The dog must have been sitting quietly at the boy's feet while she'd checked him in, but even so, she should have noticed. Shouldn't be so frazzled. She had to pull it together.

Quickly, Hayley scanned her paperwork. How had she missed that there was a service or emotional support dog coming to camp? Maybe he was the mother's dog. But no, he was in harness, sticking close to the boy, who was holding his leash.

Before Hayley could figure out what to ask, the mother turned back. "I'm not happy with the organization here. We waited in line for twenty minutes!" She stomped off after her son.

"I'm sorry about that, ma'am," Hayley said to her retreating back. No, now wasn't the time to dig into the service dog issue. Not that it was an issue, or not an insurmountable one. It was just that if Jeremy's roommate was allergic to animals or had a fear of them, they'd have to make last-minute change. The dog was gorgeous, but 'th that amount of fur… Hayley made a mental note to tell the cleaning staff they'd need to take extra care in Jeremy's room.

Surreptitiously, Haley checked the time again. Where was Stan? Her sixtysomething partner in this endeavor had years of experience running the camp. Maybe he'd know what was up with Jeremy and his dog.

Maybe he'd know how to smooth Mom's ruffled feathers.

A thread of worry wound itself around her heart. Stan was never late. What if something had happened to him?

Nothing's wrong. Just prove you can do this.

It was an unorthodox way to transition from her current school-year job, directing food service at Bright Tomorrows, to working directly with the boys. The fast-track teaching certification program, the only one she could afford, would accept the camp director job as education experience, but only if she got two positive recommendations and no complaints about her work.

She beckoned to the next family in the check-in line. "Hi, I'm Hayley, one half of the director team. And you are…?"

She continued checking campers in, trying to project warmth and friendliness and reassurance. Even though the boys, every one of them, presented a tough image, Hayley knew from other kids she'd worked with that images didn't reflect reality. A lot of these boys were probably scared inside.

There were twenty-eight of them, all in the summer before eighth grade. All at risk in one way or another.

If they had a wonderful time here, they might return and spend their high school years at Bright Tomorrows Residential Academy. That would be a boon for the school, always struggling to boost its enrollment.

Just as she finished with the last two boys and sent them along with one of the counselors to get set up in the dormitory, Nate Fisher walked in.

Or maybe *strode* was a better word. *Marched?*

Nate was a pastor, but he carried himself like the soldier he'd been.

At six feet tall with dark hair and eyes and a strong jaw, he was good-looking enough to draw the eye of every female in the room. The combination of nurturing pastor and tough veteran was irresistible.

Hayley, however, had so far managed to resist, despite the efforts of her friends to match them up.

She shoved her laptop aside, along with the confusing feelings Nate often evoked in her, and stood. "Pastor Nate. How come you're wearing a Bright Tomorrows shirt? We don't need you until

Sunday." Nate had worked with the campers on spiritual development for the past two summers and was slated to do the same this year.

"Actually," Nate said, "you need me now. Stan's had a heart attack."

Haley gasped, clapping a hand over her mouth as her stomach plummeted. "Oh no! Is he okay?" She noticed that a couple of the families had overheard something in her voice and looked back in their direction. Not wanting to alarm them, she walked around the table to stand closer to Nate. Her heart twisted at the thought of fit, energetic, Stan Davidson having such a serious health crisis. "Please tell me he's doing okay."

"He's going to recover, but he's in the hospital and facing a lot more tests. They don't expect him to be able to work for three or four weeks."

Haley swallowed. "The camp program is only six weeks long." She glanced around at the milling counselors, the couple of families who'd come back into the area. What would they do without him? She'd expected to learn the ropes from Stan, not jump in and take his place.

"Uh—Hayley." Nate cleared his throat. "The board of directors asked me to fill in."

She must have misheard that. "They asked you to what?"

"Fill in. Take Stan's place leading the summer program. Co-leading it. With you."

"But…you know nothing about it." *And I really don't want to work with you that closely.* "I'm sure you have all kinds of important things to do for the church."

He looked at her sharply, as if to detect whether she'd been sarcastic. Had she been? She hardly knew herself. Nate was an excellent pastor, full of charm, a good speaker, always ready to reach out and lend a hand. He even did a lot of the maintenance at the church, saving the congregation from having to hire repair workers. In fact, he volunteered for everything that needed doing in the town of Little Mesa.

The woman who'd complained before, Jeremy's mom, came toward them. She was definitely marching and definitely displeased. "There are no towels or linens in the room." She propped her hands on her hips and scowled at Hayley.

"They were on the packing list," Hayley said gently. "Campers bring their own sheets and towels."

"I never received a list!"

Jeremy came out of the dorm then, chatting easily with the counselor who'd helped them, his dog trotting beside him.

The counselor stopped beside a couple of other boys, and it was clear he was introducing Jeremy. The dog sat beside him, eyes sparkling, ears attentive, mouth curved up in what seemed to be a smile.

"Girl or boy?" she heard one of the other boys ask.

"Girl," Jeremy answered. "Her name's Snowflake."

The dog was gorgeous, but how long would her fur stay so beautifully white in a camp environment?

The other boys seemed fascinated by the friendly, alert dog, one of them reaching out to pet it. The counselor deterred him, gently, pointing to the dog's red service vest. But Jeremy spoke and nodded, kneeling beside the dog. First one boy, then the other, reached out to pat the dog's snowy head.

The best thing was that Jeremy was smiling and talking to the other boys. Maybe when his mother left, the problems would resolve.

"I'm going to complain to the people in charge." Jeremy's mother lifted her chin and flared her nostrils. She didn't seem to notice that her son had come out of the dorm. That, or she just paid him no attention. "I'm shocked and unimpressed."

Hayley opened her mouth to speak and then shut it again, her stomach churning. Would this woman really complain? Any serious grievance would make a terrible impression on the teaching program's admissions committee.

Beside her, Nate cleared his throat and stuck out his right hand to the angry woman. "I'm Nate Fisher, and I'm going to help run the camp for the moment," he said, giving her the eye contact and smile that made him a popular pastor.

"But—"

"Although you were expected to bring your own linens and towels, I'm sure we can find some spares for your son." There was the tiniest touch of censure in Nate's voice, and the woman closed her mouth abruptly. "Would you like for me to walk you to your car," he went on, "and you can tell me what you're hoping your son will gain from the camp experience?"

Hayley had to turn away so that her smile didn't show. Nate had neatly turned things around, putting the woman in her place without ever being impolite.

When she looked back, the two of them were walking toward the parking lot, talking earnestly.

Nate had a ridiculous amount of charm, as well as leadership abilities he'd no doubt developed in the military and honed in his role as a church pastor. He would be a boon for the program. Maybe he could even prevent the cranky woman from reporting her dissatisfaction.

She should welcome his assistance, be grateful for it. He'd showed up like a rescuing super-hero, and any sensible woman would embrace his support. But Hayley was wary of a man like Nate, who represented all she'd vowed to forgo.

Hayley started gathering up paperwork. She was worried about Stan, wanted to drop everything and go to the hospital to check on him, but she was responsible for the boys and the camp.

She thought through the rest of the day, trying to plan for the new circumstances. The counselors were already dividing the boys into groups for an icebreaker activity and then they'd all have dinner together in the cafeteria. Dinner that Hayley would oversee, of course, since she ran food services at the school year-round.

Hopefully, at some point soon, she'd make the switch from food service to teaching, but for now, during this summer's camp, she'd do a little of both.

After dinner, the counselors would have hall meetings to make sure everyone understood the rules and complete more icebreakers to help the boys bond together.

Nate came back toward her. "I think she's calmed down," he said. "Tell me what I can do to help now, and when there's a free moment, we can talk about the change of co-directors and how we'll need to punt."

He sounded so calm and sure of himself, and

his attitude convinced Hayley that it was really true. She'd be directing the camp with Nate all summer.

She needed him, the boys and the camp needed him. She should be welcoming and grateful. Should be eager to plan how to work together. That was what a true professional would feel and how a true professional would act.

But Hayley's background meant that confidence was hard to come by. And something about Nate's apparently endless self-assurance— as well as his good looks and charming smile— rubbed her the wrong way.

"There won't be a free moment anytime soon." Hayley glanced down at her tablet, which held her to-do list. "I guess just…look around for any other wandering parents and make sure there are no more complaints? And encourage them to say their goodbyes and go. I'll make sure the volunteers are set for now, and then I'll be cooking in the cafeteria. Training my temporary staff, as well, so maybe we can talk after lights out? Briefly?"

He was studying her, his head tilted to one side, his expression speculative. She forced herself to meet his eyes. *Calm, steady, professional.*

"Sure. After lights out." He turned and headed for a small group of parents emerging from the dorm building.

She tore her eyes away. Nate Fisher was attractive and appealing, and that was just what she needed to be cautious about.

If she really had to work with him, which seemed inevitable, she needed to keep him at a safe distance.

By ten o'clock, Nate was exhausted. Twenty-eight boys, all jostling for status, most homesick. Quite a handful.

He'd worked with new recruits during his time in the army, but they were *way* more disciplined than these boys. And he'd been the chaplain for the campers for the past two years, but he'd never known all that went on behind the scenes until today. Glancing over Stan's notes for half an hour had been the extent of his training before being thrown into the role.

It didn't help that his pretty co-director seemed to hate him.

That didn't make sense. He was doing her a favor, right? And he and Hayley were friends, kind of. At least, they hung out with the same group of people. She was an active member of his church.

Although, come to think of it, they hadn't spent much time one-on-one.

That was odd, because their friends were always suggesting that he should ask her out. If he'd been interested in getting into a relationship, he would probably have done it, because Hayley was pretty and smart and caring.

Caring toward other people. Not so much toward him.

He walked out to the bench where they'd agreed to meet. Hayley was already there, slumped, scrolling on her phone. "Hey," he said softly so as not to startle her.

"Hey, Nate," she said and looked up at him. "Thank you for stepping in today. You were a big help, but you don't have to continue."

Yes, she definitely had an attitude toward him. "I'll stay the course."

"But…how will you do it alongside your other full-time job?"

That wasn't her problem, but in the interest of workplace harmony, he sketched out the basics of his plan. "Church programming slows down in the summer, and the staff-parish relations committee is bringing in some guest speakers." He would lose whatever recreational time he had, but that was fine. Since his vast error of judgment that had cost his twin brother's life, Nate had made a vow: other people's needs came before his own.

There was a shout from the direction of the cottages. Not a having-fun shout; an upset shout.

"Uh-oh," Nate said, and both he and Hayley started walking in that direction.

Reggie, one of the younger counselors who stood out because of the tattoos that covered both arms, ran toward them. "We can't find the Margolis brothers," he said breathlessly.

Nate's brain and heart snapped into emergency mode as he called the sullen, almost-same-age boys to mind. "When did you see them last?"

"The campers went to wash up and then we were going to have hall meetings," he said. "Jeff Margolis wasn't there, and his roommate said he went to take a shower, but he never came back. We checked to see if he was with his brother, and it turns out Mark is missing, too."

Another counselor emerged from the dorms and came over. "They're not in the building. I checked everywhere."

"Where are the other boys?" Hayley asked.

"They're inside, doing hall meetings. We didn't want to freak everyone out, so we kept it between the two of us."

"Good decision," Nate said. "Let's split up. You two take the area in front of the school, and Hayley and I will search behind it." He quickly put their numbers into his phone.

The two counselors looked relieved to be told what to do. They hurried off toward the front of the residence hall.

"Text me if you find out anything," he called after them, only belatedly recognizing that he was using his drill sergeant voice.

Hayley looked up at him, frowning. "I get that this is an emergency, but you don't need to take over like that. We should work as a team."

"Sorry," Nate said automatically. Military personnel understood the importance of having one person in charge in a dangerous situation. Civilians sometimes didn't, and there was no time to explain. "Let's start doing circles around our section."

"You do that," Hayley said, still frowning. "I think I'll look over by the old shed."

"We need to stay together." He barked it out, a clear order. They needed to search, now.

She lifted an eyebrow, clearly unintimidated. "Then come with me. I have a hunch about this."

What good was a hunch when two kids were missing? On the other hand, Hayley worked here year-round and knew the lay of this land better than Nate did. He *wasn't* the officer in charge. She was. He nodded and fell into step behind her.

Minutes later, they crept up to the shed. Hayley raised her hand and put it to her ear, indicating that they should listen.

Sure enough, a low comment and a laugh, quickly stifled, came from inside. As did a vapory cloud of smoke.

The two of them glanced at each other then stepped forward together. Nate flung open one rickety wooden door and Hayley the other. They'd neither one thought to bring flashlights, but their phones did the job of revealing the two Margolis brothers inside, one sitting on an old tractor, the other leaning against the wall.

The one on the tractor, Mark, was smoking a cigarette while the other, Jeff, seemed to be using a vape pen. They didn't even try to hide what they were doing, and Nate saw red. "Do you know how dangerous smoking is?" he demanded. "Hand it over. Now." He held out his hand for the vape pen, looming over the kid.

He felt Hayley's hand on his sleeve. "Nate."

He was too angry to pay attention. "And you." He pointed at Mark. "Put that cigarette out, now. All the way out. In addition to the damage to your lungs, cigarettes cause fires. Lives lost and property damage in the millions."

"Nate." Hayley's hand tightened on his arm and she spoke quietly but emphatically. "Stand down. Let me handle the rest of this."

"They need to—"

"Nate." Her voice was a little sharper, and it brought him back to himself and the situation in front of him. The two boys looked scared, and young. Mark had ground out his cigarette and was stomping it, his shoulders hunched. Jeff had thrown his vape pen to the floor and backed into the corner of the shed like he was afraid Nate was going to hit him.

"Let's all go cool off outside." Hayley's glare said that she meant the words for Nate as she took the pack of cigarettes, picked up the vape pen and beckoned for both of the boys to follow her.

Nate still felt angry, but he knew he'd gone too far. Hayley beckoned to the boys, and it was clear that she had the situation under control.

He walked away from the shed and texted the two searching counselors that the boys had been found. Meanwhile, Hayley talked to the boys, sternly, in a low voice, and then walked them back to the entrance of the dorm, where the counselors had just arrived.

Hayley walked toward Nate and, before she could open her mouth, he held up a hand. "I know, I know. You think I came down too hard on them."

"You did. This is important to me, Nate. Really important. I want to do right by these boys."

And he didn't? "Sometimes tough love is the best way to reach kids."

She raised an eyebrow. "It's their first day. I don't want to start with a hardline approach."

"We need to start as we mean to go on. Stricter, even."

Rather than continue the argument, she crossed

her arms over her chest and studied him thoughtfully. "What's really going on, Nate? I've known you awhile and I've seen you working with kids at church. I've never heard you get angry before."

Her words stopped him, made him realize, suddenly, why he'd gotten so mad. He banged his fists together, lightly, and shook his head. "My mom has COPD. Years of smoking means it's advancing fast. I can't stand to see kids smoking."

"Ouch." She bit her lip as she looked up at him. "That makes sense. I'm sorry about your mom."

The compassion in her voice touched a part of his heart he usually kept locked away. "Thanks."

"And," she said, "it's probably not a bad idea to put a little fear into those boys, try to set them on the right path." She turned. "I'm going to head for my cabin. It's been a long day."

"I'll walk you back."

"There's no need."

"I'm not letting you walk alone."

She shrugged. "Fine."

So they walked together down the road, the sky a dark, jewel-spattered bowl overhead, the air crisp. She was wearing a short-sleeved Bright Tomorrows T-shirt and jeans, and when she shivered, he felt a strange impulse to put an arm around her, barely stopping himself in time.

They didn't have that close and affectionate of a relationship. Not by a mile.

When they reached her door, Hayley unlocked it and stepped inside. "Thanks," she said. She flashed a smile that had him backing away fast to quell his own reaction. She had a *great* smile.

His phone buzzed, breaking the nighttime quiet. He glanced down to see a message from Stan.

We need to talk privately. ASAP. Something you need to know.

Chapter Two

On Tuesday morning, Nate tapped on the door of Stan's hospital room then walked in.

Stan was one of Nate's favorite parishioners, despite his occasional abrasive ways. Although he was over sixty, he was as active and energetic as many people half his age, spending his free time hiking, playing pickleball and interfering in the lives of his fellow teachers at Bright Tomorrows. For the past three summers, he'd directed the summer camp in addition to his teaching math during the school year.

Now, he lay back against his pillows, his normally ruddy face pale, an IV attached to his arm.

Nate sucked in a breath of air tinged with hospital disinfectant and greeted the man. "How are you feeling?"

Stan offered a weak smile. "Pull up a chair, pastor. It'll take a while to answer that question."

"I have time." That was only partially true. Normally, Nate was able to avoid rushing through hospital visits—a challenging but rewarding part of his job. There was nothing a clergyman could do to ease physical illness; but sometimes it was possible to help with spiritual pain. The hidden blessing of illness was that it caused people to slow down and focus on what was important.

Nate wished he could relax into a leisurely visit today, but now that he was working two jobs, he had a tight schedule. He and Hayley had agreed that he'd take the afternoons while she did mornings, and then they'd work together on the evening activities and compare notes. That meant he would be on duty at the Bright Tomorrows camp in two hours.

"Thanks for coming to visit," Stan said. "And more than that, for taking over my job at the camp. I sure appreciate your stepping in."

"Glad to do it. The important thing is your health. How are things going?"

Stan launched into a description of the heart attack symptoms and the tests and procedures he'd experienced at the hospital. "It was downright scary for a while. They wouldn't tell me anything. But they're getting some test results in and they've stopped frowning so much. Sounds like I'll pull through."

"It's got to stink being hooked up to all those machines."

"It does. But tell me, how's camp?"

"Hayley and I are figuring it out," Nate said. "Between us, we'll do fine."

"Good, because the camp is a recruitment tool and the board wants to make sure it's working. We want happy campers, literally."

"Understood."

They were silent for a moment and Nate glanced at the time on his phone. He was about to ask Stan if he wanted to pray together, a pre-departure tradition, when he remembered what Stan's text had said.

"You mentioned you wanted to tell me something," he said.

Stan met his eyes for a moment and then looked away. "There's a mess," he said. "A mess I created, and I don't know what to do about it."

Nate was surprised to see the normally self-assured man looking so upset. He pocketed his phone and leaned forward. "It might help to talk."

Stan nodded. "We have confidentiality, right?"

This was a delicate question, but Nate had plenty of experience answering it. "I'll do my best to keep anything you tell me confidential. If you disclose something that's illegal or puts you or another person in harm's way, though, I have a moral obligation to protect you and others, and I may have to disclose what you tell me."

"Of course, of course." Stan waved a hand. "This is nothing illegal. It concerns the camp. One of the campers, actually."

Nate nodded but didn't speak. It was important to let Stan express his concerns at his own pace.

"Jeremy Ruffles. Have you met him?"

"The one with the support dog, right? I've met him, but I haven't gotten to know him."

"He's not easy to know. Kid struggles with anxiety. That's why he has the dog. Which... I agreed informally that Jeremy could bring the dog to camp. Figured I could smooth it over if there was a problem."

"The dog thing seems okay." If this was what Stan had texted about, it was a minor concern. "Jeremy's roommate likes dogs, and we don't have anyone with significant allergies."

"Good." Stan hesitated, then spoke again. "I was going to keep an eye on Jeremy. He's not the typical kid at the camp."

No point pretending he didn't know what Stan meant. Some kids were just sensitive, and it made them vulnerable. "He seems a little...gentler than some of the boys. I can watch out for him."

"That's not all. I'm...well, I'm dating his mother. Did you meet her?"

Nate nodded, his image of the difficult Arlene readjusting in his mind. "She seems a little high strung."

"She is, and she might not handle… Look, Jeremy is adopted."

Another readjustment. "I didn't know that." And he wasn't sure why Stan was telling him all of this. "Is it relevant, something I should know?"

"Normally, no, but this is a special case. He was adopted as an infant and it's not talked about much in his family. Look, we're definitely confidential, right?"

"Within the constraints I mentioned before, yes."

Stan's forehead creased and his callused hands clutched the bedsheet, crumpling and releasing it, over and over.

Nate's heart went out to Stan. He'd never have suspected the jovial math teacher of being a troubled man, but people were complicated, far more than they appeared on the surface.

Sometimes conversations about the deep stuff could be upsetting, even traumatic, though. And Stan was seriously ill. "We can talk when you're feeling better," Nate said. "I'm available anytime. For now, just focus on healing."

"No. I want someone to know, in case something happens to me."

Nate bit back the reassurances that wanted to

rise to his lips. Stan was probably going to be fine, but there were no guarantees.

"So, Arlene…that's Jeremy's mom. She knows I'm good with computers, and she asked if I could locate Jeremy's birth mother."

Quiet conversations were audible from the hall outside, along with continuous beeping from one of Stan's monitors, and the occasional ping of an elevator. Despite the background sounds, Stan's room felt like a quiet cell set off from the rest of the world. "I'm surprised she didn't know the birth mother," Nate said. "Most adoptions are open these days."

"It was semiopen, which means she had some nonidentifying information on the birth mother. Medical records, the like. So I had something to work with."

"Is there a problem with Jeremy?"

"No, but Arlene was concerned, moving back to the area where the adoption took place. She wanted to reassure herself that the birth mother wasn't some troubled person who was going to be coming around, trying to get in touch with Jeremy."

Nate winced. It was a harsh attitude toward the woman who'd given birth to Arlene's child, if Stan was right about Arlene's motivations.

Stan paused and took a sip of water. Tiny beads of sweat dotted his forehead.

"You're feeling okay? You can tell me the rest later."

"I'm fine. I... Look, I did find the birth mother."

"How did Arlene react?"

"I didn't tell her."

Nate drew his eyebrows together. Why would Stan do all the requested research, dig up a fact that had to have been hard to find, and then hide it from the woman who'd asked him to uncover the truth? The woman he presumably cared about?

Stan seemed to read the questions in Nate's eyes. "Honestly, I didn't think she could handle what I found out. Not now, anyway. But I want someone to know, in case something...happens to me, like I said. In case Jeremy needs to know. Arlene's great, but she's difficult. She's one of the reasons he struggles with anxiety."

"Okay." Nate nodded, unsurprised by Stan's assessment of Arlene. "If the adoption is closed, though, or somewhat closed, you should tread very carefully. The birth mother may not want to be found or may have a reason she kept it closed."

"I think she does want to keep it closed. I've known her awhile and she never mentioned having a child." Stan looked at Nate, then down at his hands, now folded in front of him. "Nate, it's Hayley."

* * *

An hour later, Nate was still reeling from Stan's revelation. So much so that, after parking at the school, he found an out-of-the-way bench and sat down, hoping for the chance to think about what he'd heard.

Stan had seemed at peace after telling Nate his story. Nate, though, was anything but.

Hayley had had a child and placed it for adoption? Twelve, thirteen years ago?

He'd known Hayley since she'd come to town to work at Bright Tomorrows two years ago. Had, in fact, been friendly enough with her to be aware of sparks between them for most of that time. Sparks on his side, at least. Though he had never followed up on the attraction—too busy trying to make amends for what had happened to his brother overseas—he'd always enjoyed her sunny nature and her ease with the boys.

He'd never have guessed she had such a difficult thing in her past.

It shouldn't be a problem for him. After six years working as a pastor, he knew that people had all kinds of issues in their past. And after the mistakes he'd made, he had no business judging Hayley.

Still, the whole idea gave him a knot in his stomach, and he was pretty sure he knew why.

And he also knew that the reason didn't reflect well on him.

Even though he wasn't planning to build a relationship with Hayley, his inner caveman wanted her for his own.

That was ridiculous. He knew it. But as he often told people he counseled, feelings weren't right or wrong, they were just feelings. The important thing was how you handled them, and whether you did or didn't act on them.

Beyond his personal thoughts about what had happened, he now had practical issues to face. He was co-directing the camp with a woman who had no idea her biological son was a camper there. Jeremy didn't know Hayley was his birth mother, either. How was he supposed to deal with that? Stan had put him in an impossible situation.

He couldn't break Stan's confidence and tell her. No one was at risk here, not of bodily harm. And he wasn't sure whether revealing the truth would help or hurt either of the involved parties.

On the one hand, he felt that Hayley had the right to know that Jeremy was her son. She'd given birth to the child. If anyone had the right to the truth, it was Hayley.

And then there was Jeremy's side of things. How would he feel if it came out that he'd been at camp with his birth mother and hadn't even known it?

On the other hand, Stan's reason for keeping the secret, at least right now, had made sense. Arlene did seem unstable. To carelessly throw this information at the three of them could result in a dangerous explosion and could put one or more of them at risk.

He leaned forward and let his head sink into his hands. *Lord, I'll do my best, but please guide me.*

He heard talking and shouting and laughing, and boys started heading into the school cafeteria for lunch.

He spotted Hayley as she walked alongside Jeremy and his dog, chatting easily with him.

The sight made Nate's heart lurch. If the two of them got close without knowing their true relationship, there could be problems. Big problems.

Whatever happened, he had to try to protect Hayley and Jeremy from harm.

Hayley sank down into a folding chair near the campfire Tuesday night. She was exhausted but cautiously satisfied.

The boys were mostly talking and laughing and fooling around, several poking at the fire under the supervision of the counselors. Jeremy, she was glad to see, was talking with another quiet boy who lived on his hall. Between them, Snowflake lay staring into the fire like a dog in a Jack London novel. Both boys occasionally touched the calm, friendly canine.

Two days in and the campers were settling in fine. Even the two boys who'd shoved at each other upon first arrival were now one-upping one another with clever jokes, a rivalry she was much more comfortable with.

The moon shone in a crescent amid millions of stars. The air was cool, jacket weather, surprising the boys who weren't from around here. But June nights in the mountains were always cool if not downright cold.

Nate sat talking with one of the counselors and a couple of the boys. Everyone had been friendly to Nate, and he'd tried to pull his share of the weight today. Neither Nate nor Hayley knew exactly what they were doing, but with a few calls to Stan or consultations with one of the counselors who'd been at the camp last summer, they'd figured it out.

She was starting to make her peace with the fact that they'd be working together for the next few weeks. Stan was optimistic that he'd get out of the hospital and back to directing the camp soon, but a little research on Hayley's part suggested it wasn't likely. Recovering from a heart attack took time.

Reggie, another counselor, was playing a guitar, quietly strumming. Boys started to calm down and, once the counselors started singing a popular country song, several joined in. Hayley did, too.

This was going well. She was going to make a success of this.

"Hey! Stop touching me!" One of the boys who'd shoved another earlier, Mickey O'Henry, a big, redheaded kid, was now standing, leaning over another boy, getting in his face.

Booker Jackson, much smaller and sporting thick glasses, raised his two hands, palms out. "I didn't touch you," he said, his voice mild.

Unfortunately, he added an ugly name at the end, and suddenly the two were brawling way too close to the campfire.

She rushed over and grabbed Mickey. Nate grabbed Booker and, with Reggie's help, they got them apart.

"What were you two thinking?" she asked the pair. "You know our rules about fighting."

"He was buggin' me," Booker said.

Mickey made a face at the smaller boy, who lunged toward him, requiring Nate and the other counselor to pull him back.

"We're going to talk over here," she said firmly, guiding Mickey to a picnic table out of the sightline of the other boys. "You need to promise me you'll control yourself and your body, even if someone does something that makes you mad."

He looked down at the ground. "Are you gonna kick me out?" In his slumped posture Hayley read a history of discouragement and setbacks and too-quick judgments.

She felt like giving him a hug but opted for a shoulder pat instead. "No, not this time. But I'll have no fighting at our camp. This is just a warning."

Mickey was still looking down, but she saw his shoulders straighten, barely.

"What are you going to do the next time someone makes you mad? Because it's going to happen. We're in close quarters here, and a bunch of strangers will probably annoy each other. Do you have any strategies?"

He nodded. "I'm supposed to take deep breaths and think about something I like."

"That's a great plan. What do you like?"

"My dog," he said, and there was a very slight scratch in his voice.

He missed his home. That was why he was acting out. "It must be hard to be away from your dog," she said.

He didn't answer, but swiped a fist under his eye.

"Have you met Jeremy yet? He's the one with the white dog."

Mickey shook his head, still looking down.

Jeremy had walked a little apart from the

group, getting Snowflake some water. She called to him quietly. "Hey, Jeremy. Can you bring Snowflake over here a minute?"

He strode over, looking at Mickey warily. Mickey was one of the toughest boys in the group, while Jeremy seemed to be anything but.

Snowflake trotted beside him, head up, dark eyes watchful and eager.

Hayley smiled at the gorgeous dog then at Jeremy. "Is it okay if Mickey and I pet your pup, or is she working right now?"

"You can pet her," Jeremy said. "She's an ESA, not a service dog. You can really pet her anytime unless I tell you not to."

"What's an ESA?" Mickey didn't look at either of them but knelt on the ground at Snowflake's level. He touched the dog's fur and his face lit up. "She's soft!"

"I brush her every day," Jeremy said, kneeling. "An ESA is an Emotional Support Animal. Snowflake likes to have her ears rubbed."

Mickey obliged, and soon Snowflake had rolled over on the ground, pink tongue out, seeming to smile as Jeremy rubbed her stomach while Mickey rubbed her ears.

Hayley let out a breath she hadn't known she was holding. Snowflake was obviously therapeutic.

Mickey stiffened, and Hayley looked up to see Nate walking over with Booker beside him.

"Booker wants to apologize," Nate said.

"Sorry I got rough," Booker said. He knelt beside the dog.

"Me, too," Mickey said without prompting.

Apparently sensing an opportunity, Snowflake rolled over, stood and then bent in a play bow, front low and back end high. When none of the humans responded, she straightened, lifted her nose and howled a little, almost like singing.

"She wants to play," Jeremy said. He fumbled in his pocket and pulled out a rope toy. He held it out to Mickey. "She likes to tug."

Amazingly, the boys took turns tugging with the dog, and when Jeremy determined she was tired of playing, all three of them walked back to the fire and sat together.

Nate stayed with Hayley, sitting beside her on the bench. "That's the power of a dog," he said.

"You're right." She watched the boys. "It's great to see Jeremy coming out of his shell. Snowflake really helps with that. I never anticipated Jeremy would connect with those particular boys."

Things were working out. If Jeremy became friends with the toughest boys, that might protect him from bullying. And his calmer manner might wear off on the other two.

Nate cleared his throat. "I wouldn't advise getting too close to any one camper," he said. It was a casual remark, but his tone didn't sound casual.

She raised an eyebrow. "I'm not close to anyone yet. But that Jeremy…he tugs at my heart."

"You'll learn to keep your distance," Nate said. "As for Jeremy, he needs to toughen up."

"He needs emotional support." She frowned. "Just because he's a boy, that doesn't mean he's not allowed to have feelings."

"I *have* worked with a lot of young people." Nate sounded either defensive or patronizing, she couldn't decide which.

Either way, it annoyed her. "So have I." Although it was mostly in the context of running a food service operation here at the Bright Tomorrows Academy, or studying about kids in her online classes, or volunteering at church.

They were glaring at each other. Nate's eyes glittered in the firelight. His shoulders were broad, his stomach flat in the camp T-shirt.

Wow, handsome. Stray, distracting thought.

His eyes seemed to get darker. Their gazes tangled now in a different way.

"Okay, full disclosure." He glanced away for a few seconds then looked back and smiled a little. "I've never been in charge of a group of teens before."

"Nor have I," she admitted. "I thought the first

two days went pretty well, but I'm still worried about how the rest of the camp session will go."

"We'll get through it together."

More tangled gazes.

He cleared his throat again and looked away. "How did you get into running the camp, anyway?"

"I want to teach." Admitting it to Nate made her shy. "I'm hoping to be admitted to a fast-track program that starts in the fall, and to do that, I have to have some background in teaching. They're letting me count this, as long as things go well."

"You're ambitious," he said, eyes crinkling at the corners as he nodded.

His approval warmed her. It also lit up some red lights in her head. *No men.*

It was a plan she'd made when she'd given up her baby. Filled with horrible guilt, she'd decided she wasn't going to get involved with a man again, didn't deserve to.

Nate was right. She shouldn't get too close to a camper. But a bigger danger just might be getting too close to her co-director.

Chapter Three

Late Friday morning, Nate headed down to the camp's indoor-outdoor pool.

Technically, he wasn't on duty until this afternoon, but one of the counselors was sick so he'd decided to come in early and see how he could assist. Although the first week of camp had gone well, he still felt like he needed to help Hayley troubleshoot any issues. Also, Ashley and Jason had said they might stop by. Since Ashley was the principal of the Bright Tomorrows Academy, Nate figured she would report to the board on how things were going.

He wanted everything to go well.

In that regard, he supposed, he was like Hayley. Once she'd explained her goal of joining a fast-track teaching program, her extreme dedication to the job had made sense. He admired it, and it made her a great co-director.

As for Nate, he wanted to excel at everything he did, which, according to his spiritual mentor, was sometimes a problem. Nate knew what the man meant. He knew he was trying to compensate for the role he'd played in his brother's death, and he also knew that no such compensation would ever make up for what had happened, nor bring his brother back. That didn't stop him from trying, continually, in everything he did.

Right now, his and Hayley's combined efforts seemed to be bearing fruit. They'd had a good first week. Since Tuesday evening's campfire, he and Hayley had worked together well. Kept it businesslike. Today would be more of the same.

Even before he reached the pool, the sounds of splashing, happy boys were audible. He rounded the corner of the building.

The large pool was indoors, but the pool enclosure had an entire wall that could be opened, giving the effect of an outdoor pool. At one end, a group of boys was having swim lessons. In the middle of the pool, about eight boys were playing and roughhousing, supervised, Nate was thankful to see, by a lifeguard. And on the other end, a group was learning—from Hayley—how to paddleboard.

Dressed in a completely modest swimsuit half covered by running shorts, she balanced easily on the board, talking and laughing with the boys, demonstrating how to balance and use the paddle. Her arms were shapely, no doubt due to her active lifestyle and hard work in the kitchens. Hayley was petite, but she wasn't a delicate flower. She was a strong woman.

Nate swallowed and looked away.

Scattered along the open deck were small clusters of boys, either waiting their turns or drying off, shivering in the cool breeze. Jeremy was among that group, and Snowflake lay at his side.

Nate approached the boys on the deck, determined to focus on them instead of Hayley. He mock-glared at the Margolis brothers, who were having words too close to the pool's edge, and they backed off and went to opposite ends of the group. Nate couldn't be sorry they were a little afraid of him. He knelt beside Jeremy. "Did you get a chance to try paddle boarding?"

"Yeah, it was fun. Hayley said once I get good, I can try bringing Snowflake on the board with me."

"That'll be cool!" Booker turned toward them and scooted closer to pet Snowflake. "Can she swim?"

Nate moved on, glad that Jeremy continued to interact with the other boys and make friends.

"You're not teaching?" The voice behind him belonged to Ashley, and he turned and smiled at his friend. Technically, now his boss.

"No. I can swim, but not well, so teaching it's not in my wheelhouse. I'll be plenty involved with the boys when I'm on duty this afternoon."

"I didn't mean to criticize." Ashley patted his arm. "You're already going above and beyond for us, and we're grateful. Jason and I just stopped by to see how things are going with your substitution for Stan. You're able to keep up with everything?"

"Not a problem," Nate assured her.

Her husband, Jason, had stopped to chat with someone. Now he walked up beside her. He was a big man, a combat veteran, and beside him was his service dog, a huge mastiff named Titan. Jason had mobility issues and nearly always had the dog with him. Ashley had hired him last year, despite their complicated history together, and they'd fallen in love and married. Now, they were expecting their first child.

"Okay, lunchtime in fifteen for my group," Hayley called from the end of the pool. She climbed out, answered questions and watched as the boys toweled off and hurried toward the dorm to change for lunch. Then she wrapped a towel around her shoulders and made her way over to greet Nate, Jason and Ashley. Drops of water shone on her lightly tanned skin.

"No, don't hug me," she said to Ashley, laughing and waving her hands. "I don't want to get you wet." She squeezed her hair as she spoke, wringing water out of it.

Nate took slow breaths and looked away. His eyes landed on Jeremy, who had his arm around Snowflake. Both of them were watching Titan.

The big dog looked up at Jason, nudged his leg then looked again. Jason glanced down, surveyed the scene and seemed to read his dog's mind. "I know, buddy. You want to make a new friend." He walked over to Jeremy. "Nice dog. This is Titan."

"Can they play?" Jeremy asked.

"As long as your pup gets along with other dogs, sure." Jason undid Titan's harness and slapped the dog's haunch gently. "Go ahead."

After another inquiring look up at his master, Titan stepped closer to the Samoyed. Tails wagging, the two dogs greeted each other. Then Snowflake lowered her front end into a play bow and gave two sharp barks.

Titan shook his big head hard, causing drool to fly in all directions, and nudged back at Snowflake. The two trotted over to the grassy area beside the pool deck and bumped, rolled and sniffed together. Snowflake gave Titan's ears a playful nip, and Titan stood and head-butted her, knocking her down.

"Hey, they're fighting!" Mark Margolis yelled.

"No, they're not," Jason and Jeremy said at the

same time. The big man and the much smaller boy looked at each other and laughed.

"Is this okay?" Ashley asked, looking at Hayley and Nate. "I don't want to throw you guys off schedule."

"It's fine," Hayley said. "We'll wait for the last group to finish and then get changed for lunch. The boys eat in two shifts on swim days."

They all watched the dogs playing. Snowflake flipped onto her back and up again, yipping at Titan. The bigger dog moved slowly, panting, seeming to smile back at Snowflake. He nudged the other dog gently with a large paw.

"I think he's being careful of her," Jeremy said, looking up at Jason. "'Cause he's bigger."

Jason nodded. "Titan does fine playing with even really small dogs. He has a friend in town who's a Chihuahua."

"No way!" Booker and Mark said at almost the same time.

Soon both dogs were trotting side by side around the area, sniffing, and a moment later the swim lesson boys finished up. "Everyone, go get ready for lunch," Hayley called. "You, too, Jeremy," she added, sounding a little regretful.

Jeremy called Snowflake and put her vest back on, then waved and followed the other boys to the dorm.

The adults followed slowly. "So, everything's

really going okay at the camp?" Ashley asked. "Particularly with Jeremy Ruffles?"

"It is," Hayley said. "He's starting to make friends. The dog actually helps with that. Why?"

"It's the Captain," Ashley said, and Nate nearly groaned. The Captain, a retired marine, was the chairman of Bright Tomorrows' board of directors and Nate knew from various sources and encounters that the man could be hard to work with.

"What about the Captain, exactly?" Hayley's voice was wary.

Ashley sighed. "He heard something from Arlene Ruffles, Jeremy's mom," she said. "She's on the board, a brand-new member, and, apparently, she wasn't happy with how Jeremy's first day went."

"That much I knew," Hayley said. "We were a little disorganized. I was expecting Stan to show up any minute, but of course, he couldn't. She and Jeremy had to wait in line, and then there was a mix-up about whether she had to bring sheets. Fortunately, Nate helped calm her down."

Jason gave Nate a fist bump. "Good job, man."

"I thought Arlene and Jeremy just moved to the area," Hayley said. "How is she already on the board?"

"Because she's a donor," Ashley said. "Apparently, she has an interest in kids who face challenges. Her son is adopted and has had some problems related to that, and so she's gotten involved in some organizations for kids with issues."

Nate glanced quickly at Hayley's face. Would she put it together, that she'd placed a child who would now be Jeremy's age?

If she made the connection herself, then Nate could be off the hook.

But she just continued walking, seemingly unaware.

"Speaking of adoption…" Jason said, "It's looking better and better for Dev and Emily to adopt that sibling group."

As they talked about their friends, Nate again looked for a reaction from Hayley. He didn't see one. Nothing obvious, anyway. Maybe a little wince.

After all, she must hear adoption mentioned on a regular basis, especially since she was good friends with Emily and solidly behind Emily and Dev's plans. She couldn't think about her own situation every time adoption was discussed.

"How are your folks?" Jason asked Nate, distracting him from his thoughts of Hayley.

"Doing okay." His throat tightened, just briefly. "Dad insists that he wants to care for Mom himself, and so far, with some help from me and my sisters, it's working."

The rapid progression of his mother's COPD

had come as a shock. Nate still could barely believe the disease had laid his energetic, nurturing mother so low. Her prognosis wasn't good.

Nate's family had done so much for him. Now, it was time for him to do for them. Two years ago, when Mom was first diagnosed, he'd moved from Chicago, where he'd been doing urban ministry, to the small town next to theirs. He spent time with them as often as he could, doing yardwork and housework, praying and reading the Bible with Mom.

It didn't seem like enough.

Ashley and Hayley had gotten a little bit ahead on the path, chatting and laughing together.

"So, what about you and Hayley?" Jason asked bluntly as soon as the two women were out of earshot.

"What about us?" Nate asked, even though he had a pretty good guess of what Jason was talking about.

"Everyone thinks you two would be a good couple. Ever consider dating her?"

"Ah, no."

"Why? She's a great girl." Jason leaned on Titan as he navigated a rocky stretch of trail.

"She is, for sure. I just…" He thought about the secret he knew. Dating Hayley would make keeping the secret egregious. "It's not a priority for me right now."

"Because of your parents?"

"Partly," Nate said. He did want to focus on doing whatever Mom and Dad needed. Between that, Stan's secret, Nate's church job and now his camp directorship, there wasn't a lot of time for building a relationship.

And that was fine. His focus needed to be on others, not on his own needs. He'd taken the selfish route before and it had cost his brother his life.

"Maybe they'd like to see you settled," Jason said.

"Who? My parents?" He thought about them and smiled. "They would. Especially Mom. She's been matching me up with her friends' daughters and neighbors for years."

"There you go. Getting together with Hayley will solve all your problems."

Nate blew out a sigh, wishing it were that easy. "She's not interested," he said. "And there are… barriers."

Jason glanced over at him. "Maybe those barriers are mostly in your head. Ashley thinks you'd be a good couple, too." He said it as if his wife held definitive answers to the mysteries of life.

"Not this time." From up ahead, laughter rang out, a musical sound. Hayley. It made him think of sunny mornings and porch swings and lemonade.

Keeping the secret of what he knew about Hayley meant he couldn't hear that laughter on a regular basis. Couldn't ask Hayley out. Couldn't get to know her better.

Confidentiality was his duty as Stan's pastor. That was fine, because Nate didn't deserve a fun, carefree, promising relationship. Not when his brother couldn't have the same.

Nate loved his work, but never before had the responsibility of the ministry hung so heavy on him, felt like such a sacrifice. And never had his guilty history filled him with so much regret.

Jason studied him, but didn't speak, thankfully, as they made their way toward the dining hall.

Nate was pretty sure the other man had seen past his words to the confusion he hadn't voiced.

Hayley couldn't quite figure out how she ended up going to dinner at Nate's parents' house on Sunday.

Very possibly, it had been orchestrated by Ashley and Jason. Probably in cahoots with Nate's mother, who'd called Hayley, explained who she was and issued a very friendly and very persistent invitation.

One thing was for sure: Nate hadn't initiated her visit to his family's home. He seemed as uncomfortable with it as she was.

Everyone—Nate's two sisters, their husbands and their kids, along with Nate's father—worked together to get dinner on the table, with Nate's mother directing the show from a chair in the big eat-in kitchen, her oxygen tank beside her. After a prayer, they passed roast beef and mashed potatoes, three kinds of vegetables, bread and a huge salad. Plates were loaded, and jokes and gibes exchanged. Nate was the youngest, and it was clear that his sisters and parents adored him.

It was also clear that they were watching Hayley and Nate. Nobody was thinking of her as some random guest. Instead, they spoke as if Nate and Hayley were a couple. Questions like, "What did you guys do yesterday?" and "How was your week?" were directed to both of them.

It made Hayley nervous. She didn't know how to clarify that they were just friends. Fortunately, Nate's sisters' kids—twin toddler boys and a pair of slightly older blonde girls, maybe four and six—kept everyone so busy that no one topic could be focused on for long.

The little dining room was full and echoed with warmth and caring, good smells and delectable comfort food, and it was exactly the type of Sunday dinner, the type of *family*, she'd always wanted.

All her life, Sundays had been lonely. When she was small, Sundays were the days her friends all gathered with their cousins and sisters and brothers, leaving no time for play dates with a neighbor girl. Some families in their neighborhood had gathered at church, but not Hayley's. Her parents, older than most others, and dedicated hippies, didn't believe in authoritarian institutions like church.

They'd spent Sundays partying. Hayley had learned young that being the only sober person in the room felt more lonesome than actually being alone.

When she'd gotten older and been sent to live with her grandmother, it was usually just the two of them for Sunday dinner. They'd gone to church, but it was an old church in the middle of a run-down part of Denver, and the small, mostly white-haired congregation had tended to rush home after services. She and Gram had usually picked up lunch from a local chicken-and-pizza joint on the way home from church and eaten it in front of the old movies Gram loved.

It hadn't been awful, but for a teen girl, it hadn't been quite engaging enough to keep her out of trouble.

No good going down that stretch of memory lane. Hayley refocused on the here and now.

Nate's mom didn't eat much, but she looked around the table in evident satisfaction as everyone else raved about the food and asked for seconds. She reached over and touched Nate's hand or arm at regular intervals. Hayley, on her other side, couldn't help but notice the affection, and it showed her another dimension of the pastor she'd known for the past two years.

He was clearly the favored child, but from the indulgent glances his sisters gave him, he was their pet, too. And wouldn't anyone favor him? He was so quick to help his mom with a heavy dish or go to the kitchen to refill drinks. He joked with his nieces and spontaneously hugged one of his sisters from behind.

He was central to this family, and Hayley couldn't help but feel glad she'd seen him in this role.

A pang twisted her heart. Was her child, the baby boy she'd placed for adoption, at a friendly family table like this?

Oh, she hoped so. She hoped so with all her heart. That would make up for all her hours of anguish about her decision.

"Now, tell me all about the camp," Nate's mother said in a soft voice.

Nate's sister put down the basket of rolls she'd been carrying in and patted her mother's shoulder, her expression proud. "Mom's one of the donors, you know."

Mrs. Fisher waved a hand. "Oh, well."

Hayley cocked her head, curious. "We're very

grateful for that. How did you get into donating for the camp?" She wouldn't have thought Nate's mother would have a connection, not until her son started working there, which had only happened this week. The woman must have made her financial gift well before that.

Mrs. Fisher smiled, but not as widely as before. "Nate's brother had some of the kinds of issues your boys struggle with. ADHD, in particular. When he passed away, we wanted to do something concrete in his memory."

Hayley glanced at Nate, but he was staring down at the table.

"Tell us more about the camp and the campers," his other sister urged and, behind the request, Hayley heard a plea to get the conversation back onto cheerier ground. So she explained the summer program's three-year history, and most people at the table listened, appearing interested.

Nate chimed in, at first mechanically and then with more energy, and they soon had people laughing with stories of their first-week ups and downs.

After dinner, Hayley helped Nate's sisters with the dishes—and dodged their sly questions about her relationship with Nate—while the men watched football and the kids ran around underfoot. Just as they were finishing up, Nate leaned into the room. "I'm going to say ´bye to Mom," he said to Hayley, "and then I'll drive you home."

"Bring her in," came a faint voice from somewhere off the house's main hallway. "I want to say goodbye to Hayley, too."

Hayley dried her hands and followed Nate into a tiny bedroom. Nate's mother sat propped up in a hospital bed, leaning on thick pillows. An open window looked out onto six or seven bird feeders, where small birds fluttered and a Steller's jay scolded. Family pictures lined a small table at the foot of the bed, and the color scheme was soft purples and browns. It was a restful place, clearly designed with love.

Mrs. Fisher smiled and stretched out a hand to Hayley. "It was so nice to meet you, dear. You're welcome anytime."

"Thank you. I really enjoyed it." Hayley squeezed Mrs. Fisher's hand and then stepped back so Nate could move closer.

"Thanks for having us, Mom," he said, hugging her. "See you soon."

Mrs. Fisher clung to Nate a little, and when she released him and lay back, her eyes were filled with tears.

"What's wrong?" Nate asked immediately. "Was today too much?"

"I'm just so happy about the two of you," she said.

"Mom—"

"It's been my fondest dream, seeing you settled like your sisters," the older woman choked out. "Now, I'm at peace."

Hayley's throat tightened at the same time that her heart pounded hard. How could she disappoint the woman by correcting her?

And yet how could she let a misperception like this one stand?

The exact same puzzle was on Nate's face. He looked helplessly at Hayley.

She gave a tiny shrug, tacitly giving him permission to let it go.

So he simply hugged his mother again and they left.

Once outside, they stared at each other. How were they going to manage this new twist in their so-called relationship?

Chapter Four

When they reached their cars outside Nate's family's house, the sun had begun to sink behind the mountains, painting the snowy peaks in shades of pink and rose and gold. Peaceful, Hayley thought.

At least, the view was peaceful. Inside, she felt anything but.

Only when she'd seen Mrs. Fisher in bed, looking pale, an oxygen tank beside her, had Hayley realized how very sick the woman was.

It was what had stopped her from jumping in to correct the idea that Hayley and Nate were a couple. How could you destroy the happiness in a sick woman's life?

But she felt uncomfortable with the dishonesty. Uncomfortable, too, was the way the thought of being Nate's girlfriend made her heart beat as if she'd just been running a high-altitude race. That was wrong, and needed to be halted right away.

A better person would march right back into the house and explain to Mrs. Fisher that their relationship was strictly business. But the thought of putting out the light in the woman's eyes—and of giving up the warm family connections she'd always longed for—made Hayley sweat, unsure of what to do. "We need to talk about this," she said.

"Yes." Nate's voice was tight. "There's an ice cream stand about half a mile away. Let's walk and talk."

"Sure." The last thing Hayley wanted was more food, but she could see how upset Nate was. She wasn't going to quibble over their destination.

"Your mom's pretty sick," she said once they were strolling down the sidewalk, past modest frame houses and fenced yards, most with people doing yardwork or sitting on porch steps. "You mentioned that she has COPD?"

Nate nodded. "That's right. She's been struggling with it for a couple of years."

"But she's so young!"

"Yeah. She has something genetic that made it come on early." He glanced over at her then looked away. "We don't have a timeline, but she's gone downhill pretty fast. They're thinking months, not years, now."

She took his hand and squeezed it. "Oh, Nate, I'm sorry."

He squeezed back and was quiet for a minute, keeping hold of her hand. "There's always hope," he said finally, "but you can see why I didn't jump in and rain on her parade about us being a couple."

"I can," she said. "She's your mom, and you don't want to hurt her."

"Right. But I'll correct it. I'll get Dad to help, and do it carefully."

She thought of the kind woman at the center of the family, possibly nearing the end of her life. Thought of the family gathered around the table. "Or…"

He tightened his hold on her hand, lifting it to help her over a big crack in the sidewalk. "Or what?"

"Or…could we just let her think it?" Even as she said it, Hayley was scolding herself. There was no way. She couldn't hold up her end.

But you'd get to have a few more Sunday dinners with a wonderful extended family.

She glanced back in the direction of the house then looked at Nate. His forehead was wrinkled, his expression serious. He wasn't looking at her.

"I don't know if it's a good idea," he said.

Heat rushed to Hayley's face. "No, of course not. I wasn't thinking." Boy, he'd been quick to smash that notion. Maybe even the thought of being with her was repugnant to him.

As well it would be, if he knew the truth about her. Nate was a wonderful son, a good and moral man, a pastor. He needed a strong Christian woman by his side, not someone with a mess of a past, like Hayley.

"I just couldn't do that to you," Nate went on. "If it were just me, I'd jump on that idea in a minute. Anything for Mom. But I can't expect you, who's only met her once, to make a sacrifice like that."

"It wouldn't be a sacrifice," Hayley blurted and then felt her face heat again. Did she need to make it so pathetically obvious that she didn't have a life and would love to glom onto his for a little ride?

He stared at her and dropped her hand, and Hayley's heart sank to the sandy ground. She'd not only embarrassed herself, but she'd also embarrassed him.

And then she felt his arm around her shoulders, tugging her closer as their walk slowed almost to a standstill. "You, Hayley Harris, are an amazing person. I don't know if there's anything you wouldn't do to help others. I'm in awe."

She shook her head and laughed, and tried to ignore the absolutely wonderful feeling of his arm around her shoulders. Even more, of his warm approval.

"You'd really do that for my mom? For my family?"

Hayley thought about what it might mean. Not just pretending in front of his mom, but in front of his dad and his sisters. "We would need to let your family know it isn't true," she said.

Nate shook his head. "No. I can't do that. None of them need the burden of a secret. And they wouldn't be able to keep it."

They'd reached the ice cream stand. Hayley suddenly felt that she *could* maybe eat a small cone, if it were chocolate. She needed the comfort.

So, Nate waited at the window and bought them each cones, and Hayley watched him and thought it through.

She had the opportunity to make a dying woman happy.

As a side benefit, it would get her friends off her case, those who kept wanting her and Nate to join up. If they thought she and Nate had finally gotten together, they'd cut her a break when things ended.

There was danger, for sure, but it was mostly to her own heart.

She didn't want to cause pain to others; she wanted to relieve their pain. And for now, this deception wouldn't be difficult; in fact, it might be kind of wonderful to play at a relationship she wasn't destined to have in real life.

She would never be the happily engaged woman, would never be the bride welcomed as the newest relative. The moment she'd handed her gorgeous, wrinkly-faced baby to a social worker to take away forever, she'd vowed to herself that she would never form another family.

It wouldn't be fair to this loved, and lost, child.

But maybe, just maybe, she could taste what it would be like. Her short, pretend relationship would be something to go on in the cold and lonely future, after Nate had moved on to find a good preacher's wife.

Hopefully, at that point, she would have moved on, too, becoming a teacher, fulfilling her dream of nurturing others another way.

Nate returned with two dripping ice cream cones. She took one, licked it. Cool and delicious.

He was watching her and there was a funny expression on his face. She couldn't interpret it.

"I made a decision," she said. "If you want to go forward with this, I'm game."

He leaned over and hugged her, coming dangerously close to smashing their ice cream cones between them. "Thank you." His hug felt strange, but good.

Maintaining a boundary between a fake and a real relationship might not be so easy to do.

* * *

Nate was mostly glad for the rafting field trip scheduled two days after he and Hayley had decided to pretend date for his mother's sake. He'd been struggling to focus on anything else. Driving one of the vans should get his mind off the challenges caused by their decision.

What had he been thinking? How, exactly, were they going to keep up the dating charade for his parents without throwing everyone else into the same misconception? And was he going to be able to put up a feasible front without losing his heart to Hayley, who obviously didn't want it?

A high-pitched sound from the back of the van he was driving made Nate brake hard. That had sounded like Snowflake's distinctive howl.

He pulled to the side of the road and looked over the twelve boys in the van.

"What was that?" From the seat beside him, Hayley twisted toward the back of the van, too.

He glared at Jeremy. "Did you bring Snowflake?"

Jeremy's face went bright red. "I…yeah, I brought Snowflake," he said. Apparently hearing her name, the dog jumped from the floor to the seat beside Jeremy. Her characteristic smile and bright eyes seemed to laugh at Nate.

Nate took a deep breath to calm his own annoyance. "You can't bring a dog on a raft."

"Well...actually, he probably can," Hayley countered. "But, Jeremy, you should have checked with us first so we could make plans. Now, we'll have to see if the rafting company has life vests for dogs."

"Life vests for *dogs*?" One of the Margolis boys, Mark, spoke with disgust. "Does that mean *we* have to wear life vests?"

"Absolutely," Hayley said.

As the boys groaned and bickered, Nate shook his head and pulled the van back onto the road. Being late for their scheduled rafting time wouldn't do any good.

His mind played out various scenarios, none of them good. What if something happened to Jeremy's dog? What if the dog distracted the other rafters and safety measures went out the window?

The whole thing was wrong. "I wish you hadn't told him it was okay," he huffed to Hayley as he drove.

"It *is* okay," she said, waving her phone. "I just looked it up. Service dogs can ride in all kinds of vehicles, including a raft."

"Okay, but first, he's an emotional support dog, not a service dog, so those rules may not apply," Nate said, keeping his voice low so the boys wouldn't hear them arguing. "And second, a raft isn't like other vehicles. Dogs can't hold on if things get rough. Think of all the bad things that could happen."

Hayley started tapping her phone again and, a moment later, she held it up. "According to this website, dogs are safe in up to class four rapids, and our max on this trip is class three."

"What else does it say?" he pressed. It couldn't be this easy to take an animal on a rafting trip.

She was reading the page and "Oh" came out of her mouth.

"What?"

"They say to introduce your dog to boating slowly," she said, and turned around. "Hey, Jeremy, has Snowflake ever been on a raft?"

"No. But he's been in a rowboat."

"Not the same," Nate said.

"No, but it should help." Hayley slid her phone back into her pocket. "Look, we'll talk to the people at the rafting company. If they think it's safe, we'll take her, and if not, then I, or Jeremy and I, can stay back with Snowflake while everyone else does the trip."

"It's not fair for you to miss rafting." He wasn't sure whether his displeasure at that notion had to do with her missing a fun trip or with him wanting her along.

He saw the sign for the rafting company and turned off the highway onto a dirt road. The van bounced and lurched along. Around them, pines, red rocks and glimpses of green water ahead soothed away some of Nate's annoyance.

They were here in God's beautiful world, sharing it with boys who hadn't, in most cases, had a lot of experience hanging out in nature. It was important to share the beauty, as well as the risky excitement of rafting, with all of the boys. Nate couldn't get hung up on a mistake one boy had made.

He was almost sure the rafting company would nix Snowflake's participation in the trip, which was disappointing in that Hayley would have to stay back. But maybe that was a good thing. Maybe they needed to keep their distance. Getting into a pretend relationship had made things strange between them. Given him feelings he didn't want to name.

He climbed out of the van, opened the doors and started directing boys to carry things to the put-in area. They'd brought coolers containing lunch and drinks, and backpacks with extra clothes and towels, and first-aid kits. Some of it they'd leave here for after the trip, but the first-aid kit and lunch coolers were going along.

He caught a glimpse of the white fur covering the van's dark seats where Snowflake had been sitting. Oh well. The van would need a good cleaning after a bunch of wet and muddy boys rode home in it, anyway.

Hayley was talking with the rafting company employees, gesturing toward Snowflake, who'd taken the opportunity to sniff around the sagebrush. Nate moved closer to hear the conversation.

"That dog's going to get pretty dirty," the young guy said, "but sure, she can come if she's comfortable in a boat."

"Is there a place we could test her out?" Hayley asked. "Like, have her get in a raft and float a bit, and see how she likes it?"

"Not a problem," the employee said. He beckoned them toward the shoreline.

"Come on, Jeremy," Hayley said. "Bring Snowflake over here."

Jeremy ran over, Snowflake beside him. "It's okay if we don't go. I'm sorry I didn't ask. I can stay here."

Nate studied the boy, sudden suspicion nudging at him. Had Jeremy brought the dog so that he wouldn't have to join the trip?

Hayley glanced at Nate. She seemed to be thinking the same thing.

"Could one of us do a test ride with Jeremy and the dog?" she asked the rafting guide.

"I'll go," Nate volunteered. He'd spent a lot of time on the river and was confident of his abilities.

"Great, let me grab a dog life vest. You two, get your human vests from over there." The guide indicated a stack of them.

Nate helped Jeremy put on his lifejacket, noticing that the boy clung tightly to Snowflake's leash, not even wanting to release it to put his arm through the sleeve. "You can swim okay, right?" he asked. All the boys on the trip had at least minimal water skills, according to the paperwork.

"Kind of. Not well."

"The water here is low, but still, listen carefully to the safety instructions," he said. "And, seriously, if Snowflake is uncomfortable, you'll have to stay back. You should have consulted us before bringing her."

Jeremy nodded. "I'm sorry."

The kid was so cute and seemed genuinely contrite. Nate clapped him gently on the shoulder. "Come on. Let's see if Snowflake wants to be a water dog."

The guide tugged a raft to the beach area. Jeremy got in and then called Snowflake to him. Without hesitation, the snowy-white dog leapt into the raft and trotted confidently to the boy. She jumped onto the seat beside him and looked around.

Jeremy visibly relaxed. Snowflake was doing her job.

Several of the other boys had come to watch. Nate climbed in, and then the guide, and they went out into the gentle water.

Snowflake lifted her nose in the air and gave an excited bark, almost as if she were proud to be on the boat with her master.

Jeremy looked proud, too, when a couple of the other boys cheered.

"Looks like she's a natural," the guide said, and paddled the boat back to shore.

"I wanna ride with the dog," Jeff Margolis yelled, which prompted his brother to say, "I do, too." Several of the other boys chimed in, which made Jeremy look even more proud.

Emotional support took all kinds of different forms. Snowflake was great for Jeremy.

Hayley had a clipboard. "Sorry, boys. We made the boat assignments ahead." Amid groans, she began to direct campers to stand in little clusters before the rafts. One of the river guides launched into a safety talk while the others started handing out life vests and showing the boys how to fasten them.

Nate crossed his arms over his chest. Sure, the river was mild here, but he knew there were rapids below. If something happened to one of the boys or to Snowflake...

"What's wrong?" Hayley asked.

"Nerves," he admitted. "Rafting is risky."

"It is," she said, and he was glad she didn't mock his concerns. "Anything could happen to one of them at any time, though, and we can't exactly have them sit in a circle doing needlepoint."

"We have to do *needlepoint*?" Booker Jackson groaned.

Hayley joked with the boy before assuring him that, no, needlepoint wasn't on the agenda.

Nate admired that about her; her easy way with the boys. He admired the combination of fun and practicality she brought to the job. They were fortunate to have her at the Bright Tomorrows camp, as well as the school. She would be a fine teacher.

In her shorts and T-shirt, she looked young. Way younger than Nate. And he would have thought she *was* way younger, too, except for what he knew about her. In addition to her directing food service, which was critical to the school, she had borne a child. That wasn't something that you got over easily.

It had to have been a maturing experience, placing the child for adoption.

And that child was Jeremy. Nate blew out a breath. He was keeping a secret he shouldn't be keeping.

A smarter man would have already found a way to admit the truth, to confront Hayley with it and gently share it. A smarter man would never have allowed the confidence from Stan in the first place.

But he was a pastor first, and sometimes, what people needed desperately was to get their concerns off their chest. Part of the role of a minister was to carry the burdens of others. To make other people's yokes easy to bear, their burdens light, because you were willing to carry them yourself.

He'd done it before, many times. He wasn't sure why this case felt so different. Maybe because he was working so closely with Hayley, and now, pretend-dating her as well.

The Margolis boys were bickering again, in the amiable way of brothers, and Nate had a sudden acute flashback of bickering in a very similar way with his brother.

His heart ached with missing Tom. And never far away from that ache was the guilt.

He had so much to make up for. He had to make a success of this rafting trip, this job, this camping experience, for all the boys. He had to do it for his mother, who was involved in funding the camp.

"Let's go," said one of the guides, and the boys whooped, and Nate climbed into the last raft and pushed it off from shore.

Chapter Five

The river was calm as Hayley and her group of boys, along with a counselor and an experienced guide from the company, floated downstream. Their raft was at the front and she'd seen Nate and his group bring up the rear.

She wasn't going to think about him. She was here to help the boys have a safe and fun trip, not to moon over Nate.

She tried to focus on the clear blue sky above, the rocky slopes on either side of them, the scrubby vegetation jutting out from rock outcroppings. The boys talked excitedly, but when they started to roughhouse, both Haley and the guide, Carina, spoke up. Carina was operating the long oars at the back of the raft and there were two paddles up front that could be pulled out and used to help navigate through the rapids.

"When will we get to the whitewater?" Jeff

Margolis asked. She'd made sure to assign him to a separate raft from his brother, knowing how the two loved to argue.

"You'll know it when you see it," Carina said. "Relax while you can, boys, because it'll be all hands on deck when we get to the whitewater."

Hayley had studied the outfitters' website enough to know that, in reality, this half-day trip was along one of the mildest stretches of river. But the boys didn't have to know that. To them, most of whom had never been rafting before, the excitement and fear would be real.

After they'd floated for a time, she looked and saw two of the other rafts coming up behind them. Nate's raft brought up the rear.

But something was wrong.

The boys in the middle two rafts were shouting at each other. The counselors made gestures that seemed meant to calm, but it was not effective. The boys seemed more agitated.

"Can we slow down any?" she asked Carina.

"Sure can." The woman leaned on the oars and the raft slowed. "At least some, but there's whitewater coming."

The boys' shouts weren't distinguishable now, over the roar of the water in front of them. But it was clear that there was some kind of confrontation between the boys on the two boats.

She could see Nate gesturing from way back behind the boys. So he was aware of the situation.

From the jumble of indistinguishable words, a repeated one was clear. "Snowflake." The dog was in the boat with Jeremy, her white fur gleaming in the sun. Was she okay?

It looked like she was, but the boys in the other boat were motioning toward her. One was waving something around.

A boy in Hayley's boat had a pair of binoculars and he zoomed in on the boats behind them. "He's got a package of hot dogs! He's trying to get Snowflake to swim over!"

"Those little…" Hayley stopped herself before calling the mischief-makers an unkind name. "That would be so dangerous."

"Water's getting a little too fast for dogs," Carina said. "But not to worry. We'll all pull off in that little cove and scout the rapids." She started rowing hard to the side of the river.

Hayley was relieved. Once everyone was together on land, they could straighten this out and she could put the fear of punishment into the boys.

The boats behind them were closer together now, and the hot dog boy was holding the package out toward the other boat, ignoring the shouts of his counselor.

"No!" Jeremy cried. He leaned precariously out of the raft.

Snowflake barked.

The other rafts were pulling up to them now, all headed toward shore, all fighting the increasingly fast water.

Jeremy started to lose his balance.

Automatically, Hayley jumped into the thigh-deep water to get him.

He didn't fall in. But she struggled against the water's strong pull. Her heart pounded with a mixture of adrenaline and fear. Could she be sucked down into the rapids?

Suddenly, strong arms wrapped around her, pulling her to shore. "You're okay." It was Nate's voice; low but clear over the noise of the rapids.

He held on to her until they were both out of the water. The other boats were there, and everyone was shouting. Shaky, Hayley staggered across the sandy bank and sank down, breathing hard.

From the safety of dry ground, she looked around until she located Jeremy. She beckoned him over. "You okay, kiddo?"

He nodded, shamefaced. "I should have known Snowflake wouldn't jump out of the boat."

"Snowflake grabbed him by the seat of his pants and pulled him back in," another boy said, laughing. "I got a picture!" The boys weren't allowed to have phones, but some had brought disposable cameras on the trip.

Hayley took a few deep breaths, looked around to double-check that everyone was okay and saw Nate, standing arms crossed, looking at her. A flash of awareness went through her.

When she tried to stand, she could barely make it. Her ankle hurt. She winced, hopped, and started to fall. And once again, Nate was there, easing her to the ground.

Carina must have noticed, because she hurried over. She knelt to examine Hayley's ankle. After a moment, she frowned. "I'd rather you didn't continue the trip with that ankle. It would be fine in the raft, but if something happened in the rapids and we capsized, you'd have a hard time bracing yourself to stay safe."

"We want to keep going!" The boys looked upset, even Jeremy.

Why had she been so impulsive as to jump out of the raft? Hayley groaned. "I don't want to ruin everyone's trip."

"We can send a truck to pick you up here. You can meet up with the boys at the takeout."

"That would be great. Thank you."

"I'll wait with you," Nate said. "You shouldn't be out here alone."

"You don't need to do that," she protested. But the guides were already reorganizing the boats, making sure that each still had a counselor from the camp as well as a guide. Nate lectured everyone about safety and horseplay and keeping each other safe.

And then she and Nate were alone, soaked and shivering, the river rushing beside them. "Come on," Nate said, "we need to be on the rocks in the sun. It's the warmest."

She let him help her over to them.

"That was a dangerous move you made," he said. "I warned you about getting too close to a camper."

"You don't think I would have jumped out of the boat for any kid at risk?"

He frowned, something crossing his face.

"What?"

He shook his head. "Nothing. I just don't think you should put yourself in danger."

"It's in the job description, although I'll admit I didn't think before I jumped," she said. Her teeth were chattering, and he put out his arm and pulled her next to him. "Body heat. It's the least I can share with my pretend girlfriend."

Oh right. She had a fake relationship with this man. This man who had rescued her. Who'd given up his own trip to wait with her.

His kindness was wreaking havoc with her emotions.

Disaster.

* * *

Putting his arm around Hayley might be a mistake.

She was soaked and shivering, and clearly needed Nate's warmth. But being this close to her made him want things he couldn't have.

He eased away and plucked a piece of river grass out of her hair. "Do you think you can make it up to that dark rock?" he asked. "It'll be even warmer than this one, and you can start to dry off."

There. He'd come up with a practical reason for her to move, one that made sense.

"Sure." She sounded as flustered as he felt. She looked at the narrow path to the high rock, hesitated then headed toward it, still shivering.

"Wait." Nate passed her and climbed halfway up, then held out a hand to help her. She grabbed it as she made her way up over the rocky, muddy ground.

Her hand was cold in his, her grip tight. Being able to steady and assist her warmed his heart.

He wanted to help Hayley. Wanted to support her.

He climbed the rest of the way, slowly, holding her hand and sometimes physically supporting her.

Of course, helping others always felt good. But would it feel so wonderful if it were anyone except Hayley?

Not quite.

Once she was atop the warm rock, soaking in the sunshine, he scrambled back down, got the cooler and brought it up. He grabbed a bottle of water for her and insisted that she drink some.

She took a long drink and then studied him. "You're almost as wet as I am. Thank you for pulling me out."

"Of course. I'd do it for anyone." Realizing that his words were insulting, he added, "But I'm especially glad to help you." Awkward, awkward.

She didn't seem to notice. "Is there any food in there?"

He dug through the cooler. "They left us two hoagies and some chips."

"I'm starving." She grabbed a hoagie and started unwrapping it, her teeth still chattering. "It's turkey. D-d-do you want it?"

He laughed at her. "No, I'll take the ham and cheese. It's fine."

They munched for several minutes, sharing a bag of potato chips as well. By the time they'd finished the sandwiches, she'd stopped shivering. Nate's clothes were drying quickly in the warm sun, too.

The immediate emergency was over, and Nate found himself enjoying the chance to spend time with her. A little too much. "Wonder how long it'll be until they pick us up?"

"In a hurry?" she asked.

"No, not exactly."

"I am. I'm worried about Jeremy and Snow-flake."

He nodded. "I think they'll be fine, though. The other boys were sufficiently scolded. I don't think they'll do anything like that again." He mock-glared at her. "You were the one who was the most at risk in that scenario. You can't jump out of a boat! Especially near rapids!"

"I know. I was stupid, you don't have to rub it in." She said the words without rancor. "We're here on the rock for an hour, at least. I don't want to spend the whole time getting yelled at."

"You're right. Then what do we talk about?"

She shrugged. "Tell me about when you were a kid. Your family seems so great."

Nate went still. It was a normal question, but for him, it inevitably brought up his brother, and that required explanations he wasn't sure he wanted to make.

She tilted her head to one side. "Did I say something wrong?"

"No, no. Not really."

She leaned closer. "What, Nate? What is it?"

All of a sudden, he wasn't the rescuer but the one in pain. It was an uncomfortable feeling. How had it turned out that she was more together than he was? "It's just...when I was a kid, it was always me and my brother," he said.

Compassion crossed her face. "Your mom mentioned she'd become a donor in his memory. What happened?"

Nate pulled out his usual two-word explanation. "Battlefield casualty," he said. Then, because Hayley seemed to want to hear more, he added, "He was scouting ahead of his team, and he was in a climbing accident. He...he didn't make it."

"Oh, Nate, how awful."

"It was," he said, and prepared to change the subject. No need to drag her into the circumstances surrounding his brother's enlistment and service.

"Were you close?" she asked.

The question surprised him. "Yes, although we were pretty different."

"Older? Younger?"

"Twins," he said.

"Oh..." The word came out of her like a sigh and she grasped his hand. "I'm so sorry. I know I said that before. But...is it true what they say, that twins have a special bond?"

Was that true? He knew it was supposed to be, and yet he and his twin brother had been so different. "I...kind of." It was weak of him, but he hated to reveal his own inadequacy and guilt to someone he liked so well and wanted to impress. "Tell me something about *your* childhood," he said.

"Change of subject? I guess that's fair." She pulled her knees to her chest and wrapped her arms around them, staring off at the river below and the trees on the opposite bank. "I made a lot of mistakes growing up."

Nate winced inwardly. He knew more about her past than she knew he did. "Tell me about when you were little," he said, figuring that was safe.

She grinned. "For starters, my name wasn't actually Hayley for the first five years of my life. It was Hailstorm."

"That's unusual."

"Hippie parents," she explained. "When they left me with my grandma to raise, she changed it to Hayley. Said the other kids would tease me if I had a weird name. Which is probably true."

He studied her, realizing how much he didn't know about her. "You were raised by your grandma, then?"

She nodded. "My parents visited every now and then, but…" She spread her hands, palms up. "They lived in a commune for a while and in their VW bus awhile. My grandma had a lot steadier of a life."

"So, was she right? That you fit in better with a more traditional name?"

"No, not really." She started to say something else and then broke off, making a wry face.

"What happened?"

"It's the school I attended," she said. "It was an academy, only not like Bright Tomorrows. It was a school for wealthy girls. My grandma worked there, so I got free tuition, but I didn't exactly fit in."

"Were you bullied?"

She shrugged. "Nothing like the awful stuff you hear about nowadays, with social media, but yeah. I had a few tough years."

"How did you cope?"

She studied him for a few seconds. "I did a lot of drugs."

He almost laughed and then realized she wasn't joking. "I'm sorry, Hayley. That can be a hard place to get out of."

"It was." She gave him another wry grin. "On the bright side, it helped me connect better with my parents when they visited. They could relate to me better as a teen addict than they could as a needy little child."

"You were an *addict*?" It was hard to associate that word with competent, wholesome Hayley.

"For a time." She stood, stretched, and then

put her hands on her hips and confronted him. "Do you hate me for that?"

"No, of course not!" He was shocked she'd asked. "Everyone makes mistakes. Look at how much you've done with your life in the years since." He was uncomfortably aware that he knew more than he was saying about her past.

His own words had also startled him, though. *Everyone makes mistakes.*

It was true, and he believed it about others, but he'd never been able to forgive himself for his mistakes with his brother. He felt the slightest brush of a feeling: maybe he, too, could be forgiven.

Hayley spun around, her clothes mostly dried, her hair wild. She grabbed a long stick and used it as a crutch. "It'll probably still be a while until we're rescued," she said. "Want to do something fun?"

He had to admire the way she could continue to have fun even though she'd covered some hard ground with him, had been dunked in icy water and sprained her ankle trying to rescue a kid today. "What did you have in mind?"

She beckoned for him to come to where she was standing, and when he did, she pointed. "Is that a rope swing?" she asked.

He shaded his eyes and looked in the direction

she was pointing. Sure enough, there was a thick rope hanging down from a tree branch.

"Want to try it?" she asked, her eyes full of mischief.

"No, we're not trying it! We just got dried off."

"But our ride should be here in a little while," she said. "They'll have towels and our packs with dry clothes. We'll be fine."

He shook his head, looking at the rocks below. "It's too dangerous."

"It doesn't go into the current. If you swing out, you'll just land in that pool." She pointed at a calm-looking inlet and then started making her way sideways on the rocks, surprisingly nimble for someone with a sprained ankle.

"Hayley! Come back!" He climbed after her, rocks falling down the side of the embankment.

She just laughed and kept going.

Nate sped up and joined her just as she got to the rope and reached for it. He gripped her wrist and tugged, ignoring her protests. His adrenaline raced and he could barely even think or speak. He just knew he had to get her down, and fast.

Get her to safety.

Prevent a loss that would be as insurmountable as losing his brother.

"Stop it, Nate! I just want to swing."

"No. Absolutely not." He tugged and, finally,

she gave in and let him help her to a nearby rock ledge.

He sat her down and faced her, breathing hard. "You're not going to run off and do something stupid again, are you?"

"Not if you're going to be such a jerk about it."

He sat, his knees wobbly. "I *am* going to be a jerk, meaning I'll stop you from taking a serious risk. You can get that idea out of your head."

She studied him and, slowly, her expression changed from annoyed to curious. "What's going on? Why did a rope swing make you so upset?"

He waved a hand. "It's nothing. Just being safe."

Realization dawned on her face. "It's your brother, isn't it? You said he died in a climbing accident."

There was no point in hiding it now. "That's right."

"Were you there?"

He shook his head. That was his biggest regret.

She scooted closer and put an arm around him, pulling him into a warm embrace. "Oh, Nate. I'm so sorry."

He let her hug him, even though he was supposed to be comforting her. He was the pastor and yet he was falling apart.

"That must have been so hard," she said. "Do you want to talk about it?"

"Not really," he said and then couldn't stop himself. "He was more of a risk-taker than I was. He served in a unit on the front, and scouting makes the risk even worse."

"Your mom mentioned ADHD," she said hesitantly. "Was that a part of why he took risks? I mean I don't want to blame him, it sounds like he was a hero and someone has to do the dangerous things in wartime… Sorry, I'm babbling. I don't know what to say."

"It's fine." Her words were actually a little bit of a comfort. His brother *had* needed the stimulation of taking risks, though whether that was linked to his diagnosis, Nate wasn't sure.

There was the sound of a truck, and then a shout. "We're over here," Hayley called, which was fortunate, because he was having trouble speaking more than a few quiet words. The lump in his throat was nearly choking him.

He'd revealed way more than he had intended to and yet he hadn't revealed the worst.

Chapter Six

After the rafting trip, the rest of the week was much less eventful and, by Saturday morning, Hayley felt reassured enough to take her day off.

Hayley had paid special attention to Jeremy, and how he and the other boys were getting along, but the scare in the rafts had actually seemed to jolt the boys into treating each other a little better. Their roughhousing and joking seemed to have a friendlier tone. Snowflake was becoming just another creature on the boys' various adventures, leaving the dog free to support Jeremy as he needed. And that appeared, at least to Hayley, to be less and less.

Her thoughts about Nate were less reassuring. He was still doing wonderful work as a camp co-director, seeming to handle that and his pastoral duties with ease. But Hayley had glimpsed the troubled man behind the confident façade, and she couldn't stop thinking about their conversation.

She shouldn't have encouraged the openness, not if her intent was to keep Nate at a distance. What had she been thinking? But the truth was, she hadn't thought. She'd simply allowed him to take care of her when she was cold and scared, and then returned the favor when he'd seemed to need some emotional caretaking.

He'd seemed so lost, talking about his brother. All she'd wanted to do was to help him, to let him be the person confessing for once, rather than the all-kind minister being confessed to.

But that had led to her reaching out to him, hugging him, comforting him. That had deepened her feelings. Made her want what she couldn't have.

She steered her car into the parking lot in Little Mesa's small shopping district. She was here to help her friend Emily, not to fret over herself, things she'd done, things that couldn't change.

And, thankfully, their next off-campus field trip wasn't until next week. Things should be calm at the camp for a few days, at least.

She got out of the car and spotted Emily and Ashley waiting in front of the small department store. They were talking excitedly, their voices— although not their words—audible even at this distance. And no wonder. Emily and her husband, Dev, had learned that they'd been approved to foster the sibling group they'd been working with. It was very likely they'd get to adopt the children. Their family was going to grow rapidly.

Their son, Landon, needed reassurance about his place in the family, and they also needed a lot of supplies.

So Dev and Landon had gone fishing, and Emily had called Ashley and Hayley to help her shop.

The three of them high-fived and then hugged. "I'm so excited for you," Hayley said, giving Emily an extra squeeze. "This is going to be great. You're already an amazing mom to Landon, and you'll be an amazing mom to these kids, too."

"I don't feel amazing," Emily said. "I feel terrified."

"How's Landon handling the news?" Ashley asked.

"He's excited to have new brothers and sisters. We've been working with him to make sure he understands he won't get quite as much attention from Dev and me, at least at first. I think he gets it, but we'll see."

Hayley watched her friend's emotions flash across her face. She envied Emily's certainty and happiness; wanted to find that love and sense of purpose for herself. And she would. In a different way from Emily, but she'd find it.

It had nothing to do with Nate Fisher. It couldn't.

They walked around the children's department, picking out warm jackets and sturdy sneakers for the two older children.

"Look at these!" Emily held up two bright purple all-weather coats. "The sizes are right and they're on sale!"

Hayley glanced at Ashley and saw the same horrified expression on her face, which gave her the courage to speak up. "Em, they might be on sale for a reason," she said.

"I don't think boys will want neon-purple coats," Ashley added.

"Oh. You're right." Emily looked crestfallen.

"And I doubt they'll want to match." Hayley took the jackets out of Emily's hands. "It's good you have us with you. Now, come on, there are more sale jackets over here, in more neutral colors."

"Guys, what if I screw up mothering the way I'm screwing up shopping?" Emily fretted as they walked across the department to the other rack of hoodies and jackets on sale.

"You won't," Ashley and Hayley said in unison then fist bumped.

"You'll be awesome," Ashley said. "It's just…" She surveyed Emily's lavender T-shirt and bright blue shorts. "You wear *really* bright colors. And kids of nine and ten usually want to fit in more than stand out."

"Fine." Emily pretended to pout. "I hope your baby turns out to love bright floral dresses."

"We don't even know if it's a boy or girl," Ashley said. "But whatever he or she wants to wear, that's what they'll wear."

After they'd picked out some bedding for the children's rooms and carried their stash to Emily's SUV, Emily and Ashley looked at each other and squealed. Literally squealed. "Now for the fun part," Ashley said.

"What's that?" Hayley hadn't been in on the itinerary for the trip.

"The *baby store*!" Emily raised her hands high. "Yes! I can get all the bright, colorful baby clothes I want, because our littlest foster, Ceci, is too young to know she doesn't like it!"

"I'm right there with you," Ashley said. "I can't pick out a ton of stuff, since I don't know the gender, but I want to look at everything."

The two women started down the street.

Hayley stood, biting her lip, looking after them.

The two of them looked over their shoulders then turned and came back to where she was standing.

"What's wrong?" Ashley asked.

"I just… I need a cup of coffee. I'll meet you guys after you hit the baby store."

"No, you have to come," Emily said. "We need your fashion advice. We'll get coffee after."

"I don't think so," Hayley said, and when Ashley opened her mouth to protest, she held up a hand. "I can't."

"You can't what?" Emily asked.

Hayley swallowed hard, looked at her two best friends, and risked honesty. "I don't do baby stores."

Her voice must have sounded strange because both women studied her. Then Emily took hold of one of her arms and Ashley grabbed the other.

"Change of plans," Emily said. "Let's get that coffee first."

Hayley let them guide her down the street. She forced a smile when Ashley pointed to a couple of hot-air balloons overhead, which she normally loved, and knelt to mechanically pet a pedestrian's friendly dog when Emily stopped and exclaimed over it. It was nice, the way her friends were trying to distract her. She knew that, intellectually.

They guided her toward a cute coffee shop, where she shrugged when they asked what she wanted, then waited at a table while they ordered for her, talking to each other in low voices.

She felt hollow inside. Like there was nothing where a heart was supposed to be.

She'd talked to a social worker a few times after placing her baby for adoption, and had been promised more counseling if she needed it. The birth center had been nothing but wonderful, with no judgment about her placing her baby for adoption or about her desire to make it a closed one.

She should be over what had happened to her thirteen years ago. Instead, she felt like the poor little girl in the folk tale, standing outside of someone's home in the cold, envying the warm fireplace and hearty meal and caring companionship of the family inside.

Hayley ought to feel unambivalently happy about her friends' joy in their growing families. And she did, most of the time. But she'd never had a strong, solid family, and she couldn't help envying theirs.

Ashley and Emily returned, carrying three frothy iced-coffee drinks. "Mocha or French Vanilla or Birthday Cake sprinkle," Ashley said. "You choose first."

"Then I want the Birthday Cake, of course," Hayley said, trying to smile.

The other two bickered over the remaining coffees and then settled down into chairs.

"We were insensitive," Emily said. "We

weren't thinking about how we have kids or expect them and you don't yet."

"It can be hard to be the one who's left out when people are talking about their pregnancies or babies," Ashley said, her hand resting on her stomach. "Believe me, I know. I was there for a few years."

"We know you'll get there, if you want to," Emily said. "But that doesn't mean you have to go baby-clothes shopping with us."

Hayley took a too-big sip of the ultrasweet beverage and went into a coughing fit. Once she'd caught her breath, she held up her hands. "You're both kind," she said. And then, because she'd been feeling a little broken open and because these women were, after all, her closest friends, she continued. "It's a little more complicated."

They glanced at each other. "See?" Emily said.

"Tell us," Ashley said.

Both pairs of eyes looked at her with kindness, and Hayley sucked in a breath. "I… A long time ago, I had a baby." She ignored their audible gasps, but when Emily reached out, Hayley clasped her hand. "And I placed it—him—for adoption."

Ashley clutched her other hand, tears in her eyes. "That must have been so hard to do."

"You're not in touch with him now?" Emily asked.

She shook her head.

"Did you get to bond with him at all?" Ashley's face drooped with sadness. She'd miscarried a baby after being in a car accident, Hayley remembered.

"I did. I... I nursed him for a couple of days."

Emily's eyes widened. She was the only one of the three who'd given birth, although she'd lost her baby in a tragic accident. "Wow. It must have been hard to give him up after that."

Hayley nodded and cleared her tight throat. "It was, but I wanted him to have the advantage of that early milk. Nobody wanted me to do it, but... I figured it was the last thing I could do for..." She couldn't finish the sentence. She just stared down at the table as tears plopped onto it.

Ashley handed her a couple of napkins and she wiped her eyes and nose. "Sorry to break down," she said. "I just... I just don't talk about this much. Ever," she amended.

"Anytime you want to talk, we're here to listen," Emily said firmly.

"You did a very courageous thing, going through with the pregnancy and then placing the baby," Ashley added. "How old were you?"

"Seventeen," she said. "That's why..." She cleared her throat. "That's why I just have my GED, you might remember from my résumé."

Ashley nodded. "I do remember."

"And…if it's okay, I don't want to talk about it any more right now." Hayley felt like she'd been run over by a giant steamroller. Her emotions had never been so close to the surface. "You guys can go shop."

"No way," Emily said. "We can order stuff we need online. Let's just chat about something else and drink our coffee and then go home."

Hayley fanned her face and tried to smile. "Thanks."

"And," Emily continued, "I know just what we can talk about, but shut me up if this is too intrusive. Are you dating Pastor Nate?"

"You're really going there?" Hayley leaned back in her chair and looked from Emily's face to Ashley's, both equally curious, neither surprised. "And you both heard about it?"

"Uh-huh. His sisters are pretty vocal."

"Ohhhh." Hayley blew out a breath. As long as her friends knew the worst about her, she might as well go for broke. "Can you guys keep another secret?"

"Of course!" Ashley said.

"Pinky promise," Emily added, letting Hayley's hand go and hooking their pinky fingers together in a quick squeeze.

"Okay." Hayley sucked in a big breath, let it out and told them about the pretend relationship for Nate's mom's sake.

"Oh wow," Emily said. "Won't it be hard to keep that up?"

"I don't know." Hayley lifted her hands and shrugged. "It was a split-second decision, and now I feel like I can't back out."

"Do you want to back out?" Emily's head was tilted to one side.

"Um, yes? I don't know?"

Ashley's brow creased. "You've been locking away a lot of your past already and adding more secrets…it's a lot."

"Secrets can backfire," Emily said.

Hayley nodded. "I know," she said. "But what can I do?"

Nate drove up the familiar road to Bright Tomorrows, but took a different-than-usual turn: to the cabins where many of the staff lived during the school year. And where some—like Hayley—lived year-round.

He'd made the arrangements by text. This was a quick dinner date to appease his family and also to discuss with Hayley how the whole situation would work.

After their rafting trip, where he'd revealed more about himself than he'd intended, he'd stuck to himself. Done his afternoon work with the campers and then left. Communicated with Hayley primarily by text.

But the upshot was that his sisters were bugging him. Why hadn't he taken Hayley out Friday night, if they were dating? Was he taking her out tonight?

That was when he'd decided, apologetically, to invite her to dinner tonight.

He pulled up to her cabin and there she was on her front step, talking to a couple of the counselors. When he got out of the car, the two counselors greeted him, waved to Hayley and headed off toward the dorms.

Hayley stood, waiting for him. Dressed in faded jeans and a simple, flowing shirt—dark pink flowers on a lighter pink background—she looked like summer. Her hair hung loose over her shoulders.

She looked her usual self and yet she took his breath away.

He tried for composure, a casual approach. He had no intention of touching her. And then he noticed the shadows beneath her eyes, the faint wrinkles on her forehead.

"Everything okay?" he asked as he reached out a hand to her. The gesture was automatic and he intended a quick—what? Handshake? Touch of the arm?

But when she extended her hand to him, he took it and didn't let go. He looked closer into her troubled eyes. "What's been happening?"

She looked away, shrugged, withdrew her hand. "Everything's fine. Those two—" she gestured in the direction where the counselors had gone "—they just wanted to talk about the open house. It's coming up in a couple of weeks."

"It's a casual thing, right?"

She nodded. "Skits, popcorn, tours. Just a way to build connections with the community, but a few of the boys were planning a skit they didn't think was appropriate."

"Uh-oh. Did you nix it?"

She nodded. "No big deal. They're going to tell the boys tonight, and steer them in a different direction. I told them they could blame me."

"Good plan."

"Thanks." She offered a small smile that looked forced.

He could tell something was wrong, but she obviously didn't want to talk about it. That meant he needed to have the energy for both of them, needed to cheer her up. His idea of what they'd do tonight changed on the spot. "Are you ready to go? Comfortable shoes?"

She raised an eyebrow. "We're just going to dinner, right?"

"Well…" He hesitated. He *should* just take her to dinner, have a businesslike discussion as planned and then bring her home.

But that wasn't likely to remove the shadows

from her eyes. "I thought we'd go to the street fair in Little Mesa," he said. "There are food trucks, so we can get dinner. But there are rides, and a couple of bands, and carnival games. It might be fun to check it out."

"Sure," she said without enthusiasm. "I'm ready to go. Just let me grab my purse."

Twenty minutes later, they'd parked on a side street. As they approached the festival, Hayley's face brightened. "I *love* country music! Is that Tres Hijos?"

"I think so." Nate didn't know the Latino country band well, but he'd read that they would be appearing at the street fair.

"I've been listening to their music ever since I started studying Spanish," she said. "I've never seen them in person. This is so cool!"

Nate just nodded, but inside he was cheering. He really liked putting that happy expression on her face. Would like to do it more often.

They listened to the band for a few songs and then ambled through the fair. It was crowded, as you'd expect on a beautiful July night. Couples strolled, families waited in line for the rides and teens clustered around the carnival games. The sun was still high, but the light had begun to glow golden, foreshadowing sunset.

"Any rides you'd like to try?" he asked, expecting her to say no.

"The Ferris wheel," she said promptly.

"All right then." He bought tickets and they got in line. Soon they were clicked into a seat and ascending slowly into the sky, with a stop at each passenger car for more people to get on.

They reached the top of the Ferris wheel and Hayley looked around. "Wow," she said. "Just gorgeous."

Nate had been too busy looking at her to notice the scenery. Now, he looked out over the mountains. Below them, the crowds still roamed, but up here, they were in their own world.

He could smell her light floral perfume, could feel the warmth from her leg and arm. He slid an arm across the back of the seat and then held his breath. Would she find him too forward? Cringe away?

But she just smiled and settled comfortably against him. "Guess we're showing the world that we're dating," she said with a wry smile.

"Is that okay?"

She shrugged. "I'm not sure it was our most brilliant move, letting your mom think that. I'm concerned about the deception."

"Me, too," he admitted. "But I saw her yesterday and she's so happy. She tends to worry about me."

She glanced over at him. "Because of your brother?"

"Yeah. That's one reason."

"There are others?"

"Well…" He hazarded a look at her. "She knows I haven't dated much. She thinks a pastor should be married."

Hayley wrinkled her nose. "That sounds a little outdated."

"It is, but all the same, a lot of people tend to agree." He could add that he was lonely, that he longed for the close companionship and human touch that happened in good marriages, but he didn't want to sound pathetic. "Anyway, my dad's happy because he wants the family name to carry on, and I'm the only opportunity to do that now."

"Oh, so we're having babies already?" She grinned at him and then her face went serious. "I'm sorry. I didn't mean to laugh when you're thinking about the loss of your brother."

"I know." She was way too kind to make light of someone else's pain.

She twisted a strand of her hair over and over. "This situation we've gotten ourselves into is no joking matter. We did this for your mom, but it seems like your whole family is excited about it."

"They are." Nate looked up at the sky. "They'll be fine, though. It's Mom I worry about. Anything I can do to make her happy." He felt his throat close up. Mom was terminal, and he'd in some way accepted that, but he was having a hard time envisioning a world without his mother in it.

He thought of his family. His grandparents were all gone, and in this region, it was his parents, his sisters, and his nieces and nephews. And Mom was the glue that held them together. When she was gone, what would happen?

Hayley reached up and touched his hand, still resting on her shoulder. Having her next to him, feeling her sympathy and comfort, soothed something deep inside him.

Their romantic relationship wasn't real, but their friendship was. That mattered. A lot.

The Ferris wheel was done loading now and it started to speed up, and then they were both laughing and holding on to the bar in front of them. The sights and sounds of the carnival flew past: people's faces, neon lights just starting to glow, shrieks from another, faster-moving ride.

As they went over the top of the wheel's circuit at the fastest pace yet, Hayley let out a small shriek, a little scared, but mostly gleeful. He looked over at her laughing face.

He'd known her for more than two years, had seen her many times at church and social events. He'd even been attracted to her. But that had been child's play compared to his feelings now.

Had it started when they'd become co-directors? When they'd agreed to pretend date?

All he knew was that watching her laugh felt like standing outside in a warm spring rain, after a cold winter. Refreshment and happiness poured over him.

He didn't need for that to be happening. It wasn't good, because of the enormous secret in Hayley's past, the one she didn't know he knew.

But tonight was about helping Hayley feel better and enjoy herself.

He was definitely enjoying being in her company. And with that thought, he reached out and took Hayley's hand in his just as the Ferris wheel topped its cycle again.

Chapter Seven

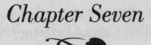

They were still holding hands ten minutes later as they strolled toward the food trucks, and Hayley's insides skittered around like drops of water on a hot griddle.

Nate's grip was strong, his hand more callused than she'd have expected from a minister. She should have known he'd be that way, considering that she'd seen him plastering a wall in one of the Sunday School rooms and repairing the retaining wall outside the church.

He was a man who could preach the gospel or change a tire or laugh like a child on a Ferris wheel. He served people daily in his work and he'd served his country. He was the kind of man she'd have liked to marry, if things were different.

She sucked in a deep breath of air that smelled like funnel cakes and grilled sausage and fry bread, trying to ground herself in reality, but it was a hopeless effort. The moment Nate smiled over at her, she couldn't help smiling back and squeezing his hand for all the world as if they were a real couple on a real date.

They agreed on tacos but as they were approaching the food truck painted in the red, white and green of Mexico's flag, Nate made a sound.

It wasn't loud, but it heralded something wrong.

She looked up, and there was Stan, on a bench.

Jeremy's mom was beside him. And they were both staring, frowning as if Hayley and Nate had committed a sin.

Heat rushed into Hayley's face and she dropped Nate's hand as if she'd been burned by a hot dish. What was she thinking, letting Nate hold her hand, letting herself pretend they were a couple on a date?

Was Stan dating Jeremy's mom? Should they approach the older couple or pretend they hadn't seen them?

She glanced over at Nate. His expression was inscrutable, and he'd allowed the hand drop, but now he put a hand on her lower back and gently guided her toward Stan and Arlene. "Hi, Arlene," he said. "Stan, it's good to see you out and about. Are you feeling better?"

He was probably right to approach them. But

didn't he realize they were compromising their professional reputation by appearing to date?

Then again, they'd agreed to enact that fiction for Nate's parents. Why hadn't they discussed what would happen if work colleagues saw them playacting?

Had it *been* playacting? It hadn't felt like it.

Arlene seemed like the type who'd complain to anyone she knew if she thought something untoward was happening at the camp her son was attending.

Stan and Nate seemed to be exchanging meaningful glances. But when Stan finally spoke, what he said was noncontroversial. "I've been home for a week now. Stuck inside, so you probably didn't even know I was there. Anyway, I'm restless. I can't work, but Arlene agreed to bring me out for an hour to see people instead of my cabin's four walls."

"Good idea," Hayley managed to agree.

"Well," Nate said, "we were just heading over to grab some tacos. Did you two eat?"

Please say yes. Please don't eat with us.

"Yes, we did," Arlene said. She pursed her lips. "Shouldn't the two of you be at the camp, supervising the children?"

Her accusatory tone twisted Hayley's stomach. She opened her mouth to explain, but Stan waved a hand. "I told you, the directors can't be on duty twenty-four-seven," he said to Arlene. "There are counselors for that. We don't want our directors to get burned out."

"That's true," Nate said, "but all the same, we'll be getting back right after we've eaten."

"You live together on the property?" Arlene sounded scandalized, and Hayley felt her cheeks heat at the implication.

"No." Nate's cheeks flushed a little, too, although his tone remained calm. "I live in town, and Hayley lives in the faculty cabins at the school. Which means she's on call a lot more than I am." He looked at her. "Are you ready? We can get the tacos to go."

Just like that, there went their fun date. In its place was a knot of guilt.

Was she neglecting the campers in her care, going out to have fun? Was it wrong for her to be in Nate's company socially?

She longed to be a simpler woman who could be on a carefree date with a wonderful man. All around them, couples laughed together in the fading daylight, holding hands, or pushing strollers, or handing cotton candy to their excited kids. Hayley wanted that. Longed for it with the fierce energy of an unpopular middle schooler watching the higher-status kids have fun.

That was silly. She had so much. She had friends, and a place to live, and a good job. She had plans for the future. She should be content with that.

But always, inside her, there was some aching remnant of the seventeen-year-old she'd been, the one who'd been willing to do anything just to get attention and affection, to get someone to see her and hold her and love her.

And look where that had gotten her.

Why was she out having fun instead of doing the work God had given her to do? Why was she pretending she could be in a relationship when that could never, ever, happen?

July third was a Monday and a lot of working people had the day off. A long weekend would be welcome to anyone, including most of the pastors Nate knew.

But most pastors didn't have two jobs.

At the sink outside the Bright Tomorrows maintenance shed, Nate washed his hands, greasy from a morning of fixing the school bus in front of an audience of campers. Today was scheduled as an all-camp workday, and he'd seized the opportunity to teach some basic engine maintenance to the boys who hadn't gone home for the holiday.

A truck pulled up in the parking lot. Jason and Dev got out.

They'd promised to come help with the workday when they could get free, and here they were. Nate's spirits lifted at the sight of his friends.

He looked at the small group of boys around him. "Okay, men. Who wants to skip lunch and paint the walls of the game room?"

"No way!"

"It's too hot in there!"

"I'm starving!"

He had his answer, and it didn't surprise him in the least. Jeremy was right in there groaning with the others, and Nate was glad to see it. Much of his anxiety seemed to be dissipating as his time went on at camp. Friendships, fresh air and a little independence seemed to be working wonders on the boy.

"We'll do it." Dev and Jason had approached during the conversation and, apparently, had heard Nate's request.

"Speak for yourself, man. I want a hot dog," Jason said. He was an enormous man, and had an enormous appetite. His service dog, Titan, panted beside him.

"We just got here," Dev pointed out, "and I'm guessing Ashley fixed you a lumberjack's breakfast, just like she does every morning."

"Busted," Jason said with a grin. "I'll work. But I'll text Hayley to save me half a dozen hot dogs."

"Ask her to save me a couple." Nate was hungry, too, but it was important to make progress on the school upkeep. Plus, he was self-aware enough to know that, on some level, he was punishing himself for getting caught with Hayley.

And he was trying to avoid her.

He led the other men into the building, where painting supplies had already been laid out. They made quick work of spreading drop cloths over the floor and the Ping-Pong tables, and then started taping off trim.

"How's your mom?" Dev was Nate's distant cousin and knew Nate's mother well, had lived with them for a short while in childhood.

"She's…okay." The last time he'd visited, she hadn't felt well enough to get out of bed. But he didn't want to talk about it and risk getting emotional. He swallowed the lump in his throat. "We're all getting together on the fifth, big family picnic."

Dev was pouring paint into a tray. "Is *Hayley* going?"

Nate looked quickly at him. "No. Or at least, I haven't invited her." Yet. He supposed he should, if he didn't want his mom and sisters to hassle him about it.

"How's that work," Jason asked, "when you're supposed to be dating her?" There was steel in his voice, and Titan, who'd plopped down on his side in the middle of the room, lifted his massive head and let out a quiet growl.

Nate looked from Jason to Dev. They'd both stopped working and were waiting for his response. They seemed to be double-teaming him.

Because he didn't know how to answer, he kept taping off trim, hoping that they'd move on to something else. He really should have turned on the TV, gotten a Rockies game on.

But he hadn't, and the silence grew behind him.

Finally, he looked over his shoulder to find them both still watching him. Jason's arms were crossed, making him look like the Jolly Green Giant, and Dev was glaring.

"You guys going to work or what?" he asked.

Dev lifted an eyebrow. "How about if you tell us what's going on first."

"What do you mean?" He was buying time to try to formulate a response.

"There are rumors flying, man. You should know that. You're the town minister."

"You were seen together at the fair," Jason added. He cleared his throat, his arms still crossed over his chest. "You better not hurt her, man."

If looks could kill, Nate would be knocking on the pearly gates just about now. He blew out a breath. "It's complicated."

Instantly, Dev started shaking his head. "No, man, that's not good enough. This is real life, not a dating app."

"And Hayley's our friend," Jason said with finality.

That was fair. Nate kept taping. "I have feelings," he said, "but there are issues."

"On your end or hers?" Dev asked.

"Mine, for sure." Nate grabbed a paint roller. "It's just doubtful it'll work out." As he said it, despair washed over him.

He was telling the truth: it wasn't likely to work out. But, more and more, he wished that wasn't so.

Maybe he could find a way to talk to her about the secret without breaking Stan's confidence. It seemed impossible, but he was motivated, maybe more motivated than he'd ever been in his life.

If he could talk to her about it, discuss the secret, was it possible that a relationship between them could work?

At the thought of having a real relationship with Hayley, cold, slick guilt washed over his body like an oil spill. How could he toss off his concerns and enter into the joyous life of love that his brother would never experience?

His dedication to making up for Tom's life meant that he could never allow himself happiness. He'd known it, but until getting closer with Hayley, he hadn't minded.

Maybe if being with Hayley would make his parents happy and continue the Fisher family name…

Or maybe he was just making excuses to let himself off the hook and get what he wanted.

He blew out a breath, unable to find an answer to the thorny issues tangling in his head.

Dev cleared his throat. "It's not really my place to say this to a pastor," he said, "but have you taken it to the Lord?"

Nate nodded. "I have. But…not as much as I should, maybe."

"Then you know what to do." Jason dipped a paintbrush in a can and started painting trim, his touch surprisingly deft for such a big man.

"Just bear in mind," Dev said as he ran a roller through the paint tray he'd poured, "if you hurt her, you'll have us to deal with."

"I will." As they went to work seriously on the painting job, Nate's dilemma seesawed through his mind.

He couldn't betray Stan's confidence. But he didn't feel right getting involved with Hayley while knowing this vast secret about her past.

Maybe he could talk to Hayley. If they took a hike together or had a picnic, something that gave them time to relax together—*alone* together, not with his interfering family or their interfering friends—maybe their pasts would come up naturally. Maybe she'd share the truth that she'd borne a child and placed him for adoption. That would be a start.

And maybe he'd sit down with Stan, now that the man was at least a little bit up and about. If he explained the situation, illustrated how awkward it was to know something so big and bc unable to share it with the individuals most involved, maybe Stan would offer to either tell Hayley the story or to let Nate tell her.

Nate had spent too much time in the military to be free with his thoughts and words. The phrase "loose lips sink ships" was still followed pretty closely by the men he'd served with. Keeping things to yourself was the norm.

But in his ministerial training, he'd learned that being open worked better in the civilian, interpersonal world. It wasn't comfortable, but it needed to happen.

Sooner rather than later.

Chapter Eight

On the morning of July Fourth, Hayley submitted the last of her online assignments for the week—yet another effort to impress the admissions committee—checked her watch, and exhaled, feeling satisfied. It was almost time to meet with the counselors, and she'd managed to achieve her goal of working steadily without thinking—much—about Nate.

After their encounter with Arlene and Stan had cut short their date at the street fair, Hayley had decided it was time to refocus on her teaching goals and forget her silly romantic dreams about Nate.

She'd slogged steadily through her online course in the hours when she wasn't working with the campers and staff or doing the paperwork required by her administrative position as camp director. Now that she'd caught up with all of that, she'd stay busy with the counselors and campers.

It was a beautiful Rocky Mountain day, warm and clear, so she intercepted the five counselors as they headed into the meeting room. "Let's talk outside today," she said. "And I brought us a treat." She'd stayed up late last night baking a coffee cake, and now she handed out slices along with $10 gift cards for the independent bookseller the next town over.

It was a stretch, financially, but she wanted the counselors to know she appreciated them. Their job, being with the campers 24/7, wasn't an easy one, and they'd done tremendously well so far.

Judging from their smiles, the cake and gift cards were a success, and they got down to the business of the meeting in good spirits. She listened to their concerns and talked through some disciplinary techniques that might work well with these boys.

They were winding up when Nate approached. He sat on the outskirts of the group and, even though he didn't say anything, other than a quiet greeting to the counselors next to him, he raised an eyebrow at Hayley.

She could read it. Read his mind. She should have invited him.

She continued the meeting as best she could, but her focus faltered and her good feelings about her own leadership evaporated. She'd forgotten to include him. Or…had the idea of inviting him flashed into her mind? Maybe it had. If so, she'd set it aside and gotten busy with other things and it hadn't happened.

After the counselors left, she gathered her things and walked over to him.

"Look, I'm sorry—"

"You should have—" he said at the same time.

They both broke off and then Nate gestured for her to speak first.

"I'm sorry I didn't invite you to the staff meeting," she said quickly. "As soon as I saw you, I realized you might have wanted to be involved. I feel awful. I know how it is to be excluded—"

He held up a hand, stopping her flow of contrite words. "It's fine. You're forgiven."

She blinked. "Just like that?"

"Of course." He shrugged. "Everyone makes mistakes, and this one isn't even serious. I have plenty of meetings to attend. Just catch me up on what I missed."

His easy attitude shocked her. Forgiveness wasn't something she'd come by easily in her life. Ever since her grandmother had thrown her out for becoming pregnant—and then died—Hayley had realized that mistakes could be permanent.

As she explained the gist of the meeting, and offered Nate some conciliatory coffee cake, she felt warmed by his acceptance. Maybe it wouldn't mean much to others, but Hayley was a perfectionist and was used to people holding her to that standard. That Nate could relax about her flub spoke well of him, and also showed her she needed more people like that in her life.

Sunlight shone on his hair and highlighted his strong, tanned arms. She could look at him, could listen to his resonant preacher voice, forever.

That was exactly what she shouldn't be doing, of course, but she couldn't stop herself, not right away.

A shout from the dorm area distracted her. "Was that Jeremy?"

"Sounded like it," Nate said. "Let's go."

She and Nate headed toward the small group of boys now yelling at each other. A counselor was there, but he was lecturing one of the campers off to the side while the others continued arguing.

"What's going on here?" she asked as they approached.

There was a moment of red-faced silence. Then, "We just wanted to see if Snowflake is a good service dog or not," Mickey O'Henry said.

"Of course she is," Hayley said. "What did you do?"

One of the boys snorted out a laugh. "They were trying to act all upset and anxious to see if Snowflake would come help them, like she helps Jeremy."

"And she didn't," Mickey said. "She's not a good dog."

"Didn't even pay attention," Booker added.

"She's trained to help me, not you!" Jeremy knelt beside Snowflake, who was leaning against him, clearly doing her job right at this moment.

"That's not so hard! She should help anyone who's upset!" Booker crossed his arms.

"She does, but I'm her priority!"

The two boys looked ready to come to blows and the counselor was still talking to Mark Margolis, who must have been one of the instigators. "I'll help Jeremy, you take Mickey and Booker," she said to Nate.

He shook his head. "I'll talk with Jeremy. You take the others."

She opened her mouth to protest.

"I can give him some tips on how to deal with other boys," he said quietly. "He may need that more than sympathy."

Her jaw dropped. "I wasn't going to just offer..." She trailed off. Maybe she *had* been more likely to offer sympathy than anything else.

Without waiting for her consent, he turned and beckoned to Jeremy. "Come on over here," he said, gesturing toward a bench. "Bring Snowflake."

Hayley took the other boys aside and lectured them—about service dogs, about being sensitive to others. She kept an eye on Nate and Jeremy, worried Nate would be too hard on the boy. But, to her surprise, she soon saw Jeremy smiling and nodding, and then laughing.

After her lecture, the boys agreed to apologize to Jeremy. He waved it off. "No problem," he said. He tossed Snowflake a squeaky toy. Soon, the dog was alternately squeaking it and lifting her nose to howl along, making the other boys laugh.

Nate gave Jeremy a little nod of approval and the boy glowed.

Hayley glowed a little, too. Nate was really good with the campers.

And, she realized, she hadn't stopped thinking about him today. Despite her intentions, despite keeping herself as busy as she knew how, she was *still* way too attuned to the man.

As the sky darkened on the Fourth, Nate looked around the small group of campers clustered outside the Bright Tomorrows dormitory building, his feelings mixed.

They'd gathered the boys here to watch the fireworks being set off at a nearby ranch. The night was chilly and clear, and Nate was glad for his sweatshirt and jeans.

Getting them together tonight had been a last-minute decision. Hayley had noticed that some of the boys who hadn't gone home for the long weekend were homesick, and when she and Nate had talked about it, they'd realized they'd forgotten to arrange a special activity for the night of the Fourth.

Hayley had quickly searched around for local fireworks displays and found one that wouldn't require them to leave the grounds.

It was just another example of how well-organized and perceptive she was.

Hayley had been passing out red-, white-and blue-iced cookies, and now she came over to offer him what remained from her container. "Sorry," she said, "you get the broken ones. The boys loved these too much."

"I'm happy to eat the broken cookies," he said, taking a couple of halves. "Come sit. It's time to relax."

She looked at him quizzically for a minute and then nodded. "I'll have to run inside and get a blanket."

"Or you could share mine." The words were out before he could consider their wisdom. Hayley on a blanket beside him, on a dark Fourth of July night, seemed like a risky move.

It also seemed inevitable, as inevitable as the

boys shoving at each other and joking around. You couldn't blame boys for being who they were.

You couldn't blame a man for being a man.

Maybe he should have settled himself right in the midst of the boys, eliminating the space for any adult interaction between him and Hayley. But as a pastor, he was well acquainted with how dampening his own presence could be. And the boys would feel quelled by having an adult, a camp director, in their midst.

At least, that was what he told himself as he took the container of cookie crumbs so Hayley could settle herself on the blanket beside him.

She wore jeans and a cream-colored knitted sweater, her hair loose around her shoulders. Maybe that hair was where the smell of flowers came from. She surveyed the boys, scattered nearby in groups of three and four, and then looked at Nate. "I hope the fireworks start soon. The boys are getting restless."

Just at that moment, there was a loud crack from the next-door ranch. A couple of fireworks screamed up into the sky then erupted in a fountain of red, white and blue. The boys exclaimed and cheered and, for the next few minutes, everyone was rapt with the colorful show.

Snowflake stood, walked to the end of her leash and returned to Jeremy, panting. "I wonder if she's seen fireworks before?" Nate said.

"I don't know." Hayley rose gracefully to her feet and trotted over to Jeremy's group. "Be sure to hold Snowflake tight," she said. "Some dogs are sensitive to loud noises."

"I *know* that," Jeremy said with a respectable amount of sass.

"Of course you do." Hayley didn't take offense, but patted Snowflake and then returned to Nate. When she got there and sat down again, her eyes widened. "Wait a minute. You're a combat vet. Are you sensitive to loud noises, too?"

Nate shook his head. "They do arouse a few memories," he said, "but I didn't get caught in the middle of firestorms all the time, like a lot of soldiers, so I dodged that." As he said it, a sick feeling twisted his stomach. He hadn't seen much conflict, but his brother had. Too much, as it turned out.

"What did you do overseas?" Hayley asked.

Nate pulled himself back from his funk. "I was a Religious Affairs specialist," he said. "Protecting army chaplains, since they don't bear arms themselves."

She tilted her head. "That's one of those jobs I never thought of, but it makes sense that it's needed," she said. "I'm sure having spiritual counselors nearby is super important to people in the armed services, and they'd of course need protection."

"Right." He didn't deny the validity of the job or the importance of the need. He just wished he hadn't taken it on himself when he could have been on the front lines, like his brother. Beside him, watching out for him.

"How'd you get into that?" she persisted.

"Honestly, there was a call for volunteers and nobody else offered," he said, remembering. "I think a lot of the guys didn't want to be around an older chaplain full-time. They were worried they'd get in trouble for swearing or be in for a lot of sermons."

"But you didn't feel that way?"

He shook his head. "I liked it. One of the chaplains became a real mentor to me and was a big part of why I ended up a clergyman."

"God has a plan," she said.

He didn't answer. Yes, God had a plan; he believed that with all his heart. "I just wish His plan had included keeping my brother alive." The moment he said it, his face heated. He was supposed to be the pastor, the one with the unquestioned faith. Hayley was a member of his flock. He couldn't be expressing that kind of wish, something opposite to trusting God.

To his surprise, she nodded. "It's hard to know what He has in mind sometimes." She put a hand over his and squeezed, briefly.

The touch felt like a balm of reassurance. He

could let down his guard around her. He didn't have to be the perfect pastor.

It looked like she was winding up to ask another question, so he was glad when an especially spectacular firework erupted across the sky, causing everyone to ooh and aah.

Everyone, that is, except the group Jeremy was with. They'd moved off to one side and were talking, laughing and bending together over something.

A moment later, there was a whoosh and a flash that had them all jumping back, hooting and high-fiving each other.

Nate was on his feet and marching over before the dust had settled. "What's going on?"

The boys looked abashed. "We, uh, we kinda made a bottle rocket," one of them said.

"I did it." Jeremy was confessing, but there was pride in his voice. "I figured it out in science class last year."

Nate's eyes narrowed. "Where did you get your supplies?" he asked, kneeling beside the heap of foil squares, wooden skewers and electrical tape in the center of the boys' circle.

"It's just household stuff," Jeremy said. "I borrowed it from the kitchen."

A couple of the boys giggled.

Nate frowned. What Jeremy had done was

dangerous, but it was good to see him making friends.

Hayley came over then, and Nate was glad to have her approach so that he wouldn't have to deal with all of this alone. He couldn't figure out what an appropriate consequence would be, and Hayley tended to be great at that.

"Where's Snowflake?" she asked.

Nate looked around and didn't see her. "Did you put her inside?" he asked Jeremy.

"No." Jeremy's face was stricken. "She was right here. I... I must have let go of her leash. Snowflake! Come!" He let out a loud whistle.

No sign of the white dog. More whistles and yells didn't bring her running either.

Nate glanced at Hayley. "We'd better start hunting. You take one group of boys and I'll take the other."

"Oh no. Oh no." Jeremy's voice was tight, his face screwed up in an effort not to cry. "I let her go. I lost her. Snowflake!"

Nate glanced at Hayley. "Come on," he said to a group of four other boys. "We'll cover the area to the right. Hayley will take the left side with her crew." In this situation, with Jeremy so upset, he deemed it best to let Hayley deal with Jeremy. She'd probably manage his feelings better than Nate would.

Because she's his mother.

Nate winced and pushed the thought aside. He took his group over the hillside and they fanned out, staying in sight of one another at Nate's insistence.

Ten minutes later, they gathered back at the group area, where the grand finale from the firework display at the neighboring ranch was just going off.

"She'll be so scared of all the noise." Jeremy was openly sobbing now. "Why did I let her go?"

"Everyone makes mistakes," Nate reminded him.

"Nate, could you and Jeremy hunt inside while the rest of us go on looking out here?" Hayley gave him a meaningful gaze.

"Of course." She must want him to get Jeremy out of the public eye, since big meltdowns weren't something boys wanted other boys to see. But practicality compelled him to add, "Is there really a chance she could she be inside, though?"

"People have been in and out of the dorm," Hayley said. "It's possible she ran in when one of them opened the door."

"When I went in to use the bathroom, the door was propped open," Mark Margolis volunteered. "We're supposed to close the door but someone—" he glared at his brother "—left it open."

"Ah."

"I have a feeling," Hayley said. "I think you

should look." She didn't say anything more about what the feeling was, but having experienced its power finding the boys who'd been smoking, Nate wasn't about to argue with Hayley's intuitions.

"Let's go," he said to Jeremy, and they headed inside.

The boy was still gasping and sobbing. "I shouldn't have let her go," he kept repeating.

Nate put a hand on Jeremy's shoulder. "No, you shouldn't have, and you shouldn't have made the bottle rockets either. But even if something happened to Snowflake, it doesn't mean you're a horrible person. Just that you screwed up, like we all do."

As he said it, he felt a little shiver, like a whisper from God.

Was the claim he'd just made true for him, too? Even if something had happened to his brother—which it had—it didn't mean Nate was a horrible person. Just that he'd screwed up.

He set that thought aside to deal with later. "Where would Snowflake have gone?" he asked.

Jeremy cleared his throat and wiped his face on his sleeve. "The lounge? There's usually some snacks in there."

"Let's go."

They hunted the lounges on each floor, but although Jeremy crawled around to look under every piece of furniture, the white dog was nowhere to be found.

"Do you have treats for her?" Nate asked. "Maybe if she hears you shaking the box, she'll come out. If it doesn't work inside, we'll do it outside."

"They're in my room."

Nate followed the boy upstairs and winced at the dirty socks, empty potato chip bags and drawing supplies that covered the floor. Jeremy dug through a pile of clothes in the closet and finally came up with a box of dog biscuits. "Here they are!"

"We'll walk around shaking them," Nate suggested.

Just then, a quiet whine sounded from the other side of the room.

Nate and Jeremy looked at each other. "Was that her?" Nate asked.

"Snowflake! Here, girl, where are you?"

The white dog eased herself out of the narrow space under Jeremy's bed and ran to him, tail wagging.

"Snowflake!" The boy knelt and buried his face in her fur. "You're here! You came back to the room! You're safe!" He was laughing and crying at the same time.

Snowflake plowed into Jeremy over and over,

bumping him with her head, knocking him down, even lifting her muzzle to howl a little.

Their joy in being back together was a beautiful sight.

Nate had to force himself to stop taking it in long enough to pull out his phone and text Hayley.

Found Snowflake inside.

His phone buzzed immediately with an incoming call. "You found her? She's okay?"

"She's fine, and so is Jeremy. We're in his room."

"I'll herd the boys inside and meet you downstairs. I want to hear all about it."

Fireworks went off inside Nate's chest. She wanted to meet up with him and talk to him. And he wanted nothing more than to tell her about it, to see her happiness, to be with her.

An hour later, the boys were settled down and in their rooms. Nate walked Hayley back to her cabin.

And then he found that he didn't want to leave.

They'd been chatting casually about what had happened with Snowflake, but that conversation had come to its natural end. Now, she turned and looked up at him, her expression suddenly cautious.

"Seems a shame to go home so early on the Fourth of July," he risked saying. "Would you want to sit outside and look at the stars?"

Great job, Fisher. Sounds like the worst pickup line ever.

She tilted her head to one side, studying him as if she could discern his intent that way.

"I really do mean just look at the stars," he said.

"In that case, have a seat." She gestured to the swing on her porch. "I'll bring us out some sodas."

The fact that she was letting him stay sent hope soaring through him, as high and wild as an eagle's flight. Probably the wrong thing to feel, considering she'd only said yes when he'd clarified that he wasn't looking for romance but just some stargazing.

She'd made it plain that she didn't want anything more, and a decent, good man would accept that and move on. But Nate wasn't really looking for romance either. Or rather, he wasn't looking for it purposefully, and he wouldn't follow through if he got the chance. His focus had to be on work and service, not the pleasures of a wife and family.

Still, when she came back out onto the porch with two glasses of orange soda on ice—his favorite, which she must have noticed during group gatherings—she seemed to glow like a beautiful beacon of all he'd ever wanted.

She hesitated before sitting on the swing. Pressed as far away from him as she could be.

That was a clear signal, for sure. But they could still have a friendly conversation, right? "You told me a little about your childhood before, but I'd like to hear more, if you don't mind sharing."

He figured that knowing more about her might quell his desire to get closer. After all, he knew what she didn't know he knew: she'd had a baby and placed it for adoption. Maybe if she told him something about that, he'd realize she wasn't the woman for him, contrary to what his heart said.

She looked at him searchingly and then away, staring out into the darkness. Overhead, the stars were bright and plentiful, and far, far away. A gentle breeze brought the fragrance of sage and the ponderosa pines that dotted the Bright Tomorrows landscape.

"My past is bad," she said finally in a flat voice.

Maybe digging into her history wasn't a good idea. "You don't have to—"

"I mentioned that I got into drugs," she interrupted. "Got in with a bad crowd and went out of control."

"It happens. But that must have been tough."

Even though he was vehemently antidrug and avoided alcohol, due to his upbringing and his time in street ministry, he found that he didn't feel put off by her past. He just felt more sympathetic. "How did you get past it?"

"I never did a twelve-step program or anything. I was kind of…jolted out of it."

"Do you want to talk about it?" Nate's heart was pounding. Was she going to reveal what had happened?

She was still staring out into the darkness. "My grandmother, who mostly raised me…well, some stuff happened, and she kicked me out. Which was totally justified, although I didn't see it that way at the time. And then…" She stopped speaking abruptly, her head bowing.

She'd stopped clinging to the edge of the swing while she'd talked, and now he reached out and put an arm around her shoulders. "It's okay. You don't have to talk about it."

"I need to," she said. "She…she died. Before I could apologize to her for the awful things I'd said and done. Before I could thank her for raising me when my parents bailed on the job." Her voice sounded tight, like she was forcing out the words.

He squeezed her shoulder a little and then let go. He wanted to comfort her, but the dynamic between them was different than it would be if she were a guy or an older parishioner or…well, anyone else.

He was too attracted to Hayley to be able to put his arm around her without thinking about possibilities that could never come true.

Couldn't they? Maybe?

"That must have been hard to deal with," he said quietly, keeping his hands at his sides and reaching for his professional counseling techniques. "I'm guessing she knew you loved her and that anything bad you said came from the drugs and from being an adolescent, not from your heart."

"I hope so," she said, her eyes shining with unshed tears. "We didn't have the perfect relationship, but I… The older I get, the more I realize how much she sacrificed for me. I had no idea at the time. I just felt embarrassed that my grandma wore old-fashioned clothes and shoes and came to every single open house or teacher event when half the other parents had stopped showing up." Her voice thickened and one tear rolled down her cheek. "I didn't know enough to be thankful."

Why wasn't he the kind of guy who carried a handkerchief? "Let me run in and grab you some tissues, is that okay?"

She nodded and he dashed inside and located the bathroom, where he found a box of tissues.

As he walked through her cabin on the way to the porch, he noticed the embroidered pillows on the couch and the teaching books piled up beside an armchair. When he saw the Bible open on the dining room table with what looked like a journal beside it, he turned away quickly, feeling like he'd invaded her privacy.

He was also ashamed of himself. He'd expected her to tell him about her pregnancy and had thought maybe that would turn him off from caring about her. But she was simply a struggling child of God, as he was. She'd made mistakes, as he had. And she'd suffered through pain and guilt that obviously still affected her. The right response was compassion, not judgment.

He brought the tissues outside and she wiped her eyes and then looked over at him with a sad attempt at a laugh. "Sorry. You weren't counting on a breakdown when you said you wanted to gaze at the stars."

He took her hand between his own, leaning forward, not looking at her. "I'm glad for the chance to know you better," he said. "And I'm sorry you went through that."

"Don't be sorry for me. I brought it on myself."

He shook his head. "I'm sure there's some of that. We all have free will. But I'm hearing about a girl whose parents let her down and whose childhood was lonely. That wasn't your fault."

Her smile was watery but real. "You're the type to see the best in other people, aren't you?"

He shrugged. "We're all flawed, present company included, but you have a lot of strengths," he said. "There's a lot to...to like about you, Hayley." He'd had to stop himself then because he'd almost said "love." And it was true, there was a lot to love about Hayley.

She hadn't told him about the pregnancy and adoption, though, and he certainly didn't have the right to push her into a confession like that. Especially not when she was emotional from the other truths she'd revealed.

She was looking at him. "Thank you for being kind," she said, and this time she didn't look away. Her hand still between his, she reached out with her other hand, squeezing his.

He couldn't look away. Could not. Even a raging forest fire wouldn't have been able to distract his attention from her warm eyes. They were gray, he knew that, but in the dimness, they shone almost silver.

He extricated one of his hands and reached up to touch her face, drawn almost irresistibly, like there was a magnet attracting him.

She sucked in an audible breath and then turned her face into his palm, letting him cup it.

He felt each pore of her skin, each breath she

took. His whole being hummed at this new closeness between them.

It was Hayley who broke away first. She didn't lean away, but rather forward. "Look out there," she said.

With an effort, he did, and was rewarded with the sight of a pair of mule deer, silvery in the starlight, nibbling on a low bush across the road from her cabin.

"Wow," he said.

"Yeah. They're out there most nights."

"The same pair?"

"Uh-huh. I'm pretty sure."

Nate watched the deer, or tried to, but his thoughts took the sight in a whole different direction. They were beautiful animals, but even sweeter was that they were together, buck and doe, bonded in the silvery starlight.

Nate wanted to be bonded, too. He hadn't been this close with a woman in…well, ever. Not really. He and Hayley had worked together and laughed together and prayed together. Now they'd cried together.

Longing rose in him, so intense that it nearly pressed him back in the swing. He wanted more than friendship with her; he wanted a relationship. To be a man and a woman together.

Of its own volition, or so it seemed, his arm slid around her shoulders and he tugged her a few inches closer. She made a tiny sound in her throat, ambiguous—was it protest or affirmation? He used his other hand to brush back her hair, trying to read her expression.

"Nate…" She was staring at him again, her eyes enormous.

"Is this too much?" *Please say no. Please.*

She stared at him for a moment longer. Then, slowly, she shook her head.

There were all kinds of reasons he should back away, but right now he couldn't think of any of them. Instead, he gave in to the emotions raging through his blood.

He pulled her into his arms and kissed her.

Chapter Nine

The tenderness of Nate's kiss melted Hayley, allowing her to relax into his arms.

This was *Nate*. A good man, one who wouldn't take advantage.

She was unused to kissing, just like she was unused to being with a man, but it must be like riding a bike: you never forgot how.

Or…no, that was wrong, because kissing Nate was completely different from the kisses of her teenage years. Even when his gentle touch intensified, making her insides sizzle, it wasn't like the other times. It was tender and respectful and *right*.

At least, it could have been right, if she hadn't screwed up her life too badly for any man to care for her. Too badly to have the right for a loving relationship.

And she was going to pull away. Soon. Very

soon. Just as soon as she'd taken the opportunity to put her hands on his muscular shoulders, to bask in the strength of his arms.

He pulled her gently into his chest and rested his cheek on the top of her hand. "Hayley, Hayley. I didn't mean to do that, but I'm not sorry I did."

"I'm not either," she admitted. "I guess our fake relationship just got real."

"I guess it did." He let her out of his arms, seeming reluctant to do it, and then leaned back far enough to study her face. "We should probably talk about what this could mean."

It can't mean anything. The reality of her life and her decisions tried to seep back in around the edges of her joy. But she didn't want it here. Didn't want anything to take away from the sweet feeling she'd gotten from his embrace and his kiss. "Not tonight," she said. "Please, not tonight."

"Okay." He was studying her speculatively, and suddenly she felt vulnerable. Like he could read her, at least a little. But she also felt vulnerable because she was a woman alone with a man in a very tempting situation. Nate was a good man, more than good; he was a man of God.

But he was still a man.

"You should go," she said and stood. "And I should go inside."

He looked like he was going to argue. His brown eyes held emotions that ran deep and complicated. His eyes drew her, with their beauty and their kindness, but they also awakened her conscience. He shouldn't be toyed with if she could never take their relationship to any kind of conclusion.

She backed away from him, unable to stop looking. She wanted to freeze this moment in time. To remember his slightly mussed hair and his breathing, a little thicker than normal. To feel the burning effect of his gaze.

Just for tonight, she wanted to pretend that something between them could work. So she stepped forward and dropped a quick kiss on his stubbled cheek and then darted back out of the reach of his arms.

"Talk tomorrow," she said.

The next morning, the idea of talking about what it could all mean was even less appealing. Hayley hadn't slept well. She'd been wrestling with her feelings: joy with shame, guilt with excitement.

Before they'd kissed, she had been able to enjoy her attraction to Nate without naming it or worrying too much about its implications. It had been an innocent daydream, like that of a girl reading a princess story.

Now everything was different. Now she'd tasted what it felt like to be a woman with Nate, a grown-up woman with a grown-up man.

She'd liked it. Wanted it to continue. Longing she hadn't known was inside her had come unleashed, and she was having trouble scolding it back into its closed box.

It would have been easier to handle if they could have had some time apart, so she could bring her heart back under control. But that wasn't possible because today was the gathering with his family, and she'd agreed to go.

She wished like anything she hadn't. But they'd let the counselors know they'd be gone all day, and the counselors had embraced the opportunity to be in charge. It would almost be more trouble, and would definitely require too many awkward explanations, to back out now.

"You look tired," Nate said when she got in his truck.

"Thanks a lot," she said, deliberately grouchy. "Don't you know that's as much as saying I look awful?"

"I didn't mean…" He trailed off.

"I know what you meant," she snapped.

He winced. "Sorry," he said, raising both hands, palms out.

"It's fine." But it wasn't. She wanted to look good, not tired. She wanted to know whether he'd slept well, whether he'd dwelt on their kiss as she had.

As he pulled out and headed down the road from her cabin, she crossed her arms and studied her phone, not talking.

Unfortunately, she couldn't stop herself from thinking. About how handsome he was, about how he'd wrapped her in his arms, about how respectful he'd been, not pushing any boundaries with their kiss.

She wanted to forget, but that wasn't going to be easy.

After five minutes of silence, he cleared his throat. "Sometimes, when people are unsure how to handle a situation or relationship, they pick a fight," he said. "I wonder if that's what you're doing."

"Mr. Know-it-all," she grumbled.

"If you didn't want to come, you should have said so."

"Who's picking a fight now?" she asked.

"Sorry. You're right."

His easy acquiescence made Hayley feel guilty. "I'm sorry. I'm just…you're right, I *am* tired. And I *don't* know how to handle this situation."

"I don't either." He sighed. "I'm not going to lie. I loved kissing you. But it was a mistake."

His words made her heart leap and pound

harder. She felt the same way, but there was a part of her that wished he was unambiguously happy about their kiss. "You're probably right," she said.

"We're still friends though, right?" He reached out and clasped her fingers, just briefly.

His touch had an impact that was definitely not just friend-like. "Yeah. Of course."

"So maybe we should just put thinking or talking about it on hold for today, or at least, for the length of time we're with my family. It's…" He sighed. "It's not going to be an easy day, aside from any difficulties between us."

That didn't sound good. "You were vague about what today's event even is." Beyond telling her to dress casually, he'd seemed to evade her questions.

"Uh, yeah." He turned down a small side road. "It's actually a birthday party."

"Oh, for whom?" Hayley was distressed. "I didn't get a present."

"It's, uh, for me." He turned again.

Now she really felt bad, not having known it was his birthday, not having gotten him a gift. But it did clear up her confusion about why the family was gathering on the day after the 4th, rather than on the holiday itself. She looked out the window as the car slowed.

White gravestones, dozens of them, beside a

small country church. "Wait, we're going to a birthday party at a cemetery?"

He nodded.

"Why?"

He pulled into the gravel parking lot and glanced over. "It's my birthday, but also my brother's."

"Whoa." She wanted to question him more, but there were a couple of cars and an SUV up ahead, a cluster of people. Someone was helping Mrs. Fisher out of her car, unfolding a wheelchair for her. Someone else was spreading a picnic blanket.

As soon as Hayley got out of the car, Mrs. Fisher beckoned her over. "I'm sure our tradition must seem strange to you, dear," she said. "We've been doing it ever since Nate moved back and Tom…well, since he left us."

"It's fine, I just wish I'd known. I didn't even buy Nate a gift."

His mother studied her, eyes sharp, and Hayley felt self-conscious. She was a bad girlfriend. A bad pretend girlfriend.

Nate rescued her by asking her if she'd get everyone drinks from the cooler he'd brought. Soon they were all settling down to eat delicious sandwiches, fruit and cake. They talked about Nate's brother and prayed. Discussed how he was happier now with Jesus, because he'd been a Christian—not a conventional one, but he'd believed. They shared funny stories about him, each one prompting laughter and reminding someone of another anecdote to share.

What a strange world. This family, close and connected, and everything Hayley had ever wanted, spent their living son's birthday focused on the son they'd lost. Nate seemed to take it in stride, but Hayley watched his face and wondered.

The sun rose higher in the sky and Nate and his sisters and father went over to an adjoining field to play softball. Hayley offered to stay with Nate's mother, who looked pleased and agreed.

"So I have a question," Hayley said after the others were out of earshot. "Does Nate ever get a happier birthday party?"

"This isn't…" Nate's mother looked around a little. "This isn't actually unhappy to us, but I see what you mean. It's keeping his birthday tied to a sad occasion."

"It's probably sort of inevitable, them being twins, but maybe…" Hayley let her words fall away.

"Go ahead. You can say it."

"I just thought…maybe something more festive would be good for him."

"More festive than a cemetery?" Mrs. Fisher patted Hayley's hand. "I'm so glad you're together. We need an outside perspective. You're good for Nate."

Hayley's stomach twisted. She wanted to be good for Nate and was pleased his mother thought she was. At the same time, if his family knew everything about her…knew what kind of a person she'd been, what she'd done, they'd have an entirely different attitude.

When Nate and his sisters came back over to start gathering things up to load into the cars, Nate's mother grabbed two metal serving spoons and banged them together. "Okay, everyone, I have a couple of announcements," she said. "First off, I do *not* want you doing this for me when I'm gone. No cemetery parties."

There were murmurs and hugs, and someone said "You're going to be fine," but the woman's face settled into determined lines and she shook her head. "I'm *not* going to be fine. Whenever I pass on—and that timeline is in the Lord's hands—you're to bury me respectfully and then go on to have happy lives full of fun." Looking around, she must have seen the stricken expressions on so many faces. "I'll be celebrating, too," she said quietly. "Me and Tommy. We'll be with Jesus, and we'll see you all again."

There was lots of hugging then. But Mrs. Fisher wasn't finished. "One more thing. We're having a fish fry for Nate's birthday tonight. A real party." She pointed at Nate and then at his father. "And I expect you two men to catch us some nice trout, understand?"

Nate glanced quickly at Hayley and she read his question and gave a quick nod.

She hadn't expected the event to go on all day, nor to spend time with Nate's family without Nate. But she was growing more and more fond of them, and she wanted to support his mother in her wishes.

As they were packing up the cars, Nate took her hand and tugged her aside. "Are you sure this is okay? I can run you home if you don't want to stay."

What she *wanted* was to stay with her hand in his, forever, feeling the strength of it, relishing the closeness. "I'll be fine," she said, her voice coming out husky. "I want to stay."

As Nate and his father made their way down to one of their favorite fishing streams, Nate's thoughts were a chaotic tangle.

Everything mingled in him. His guilt that he and his father hadn't fished here together for more than a year, due to Nate's being overly busy and his father not wanting anyone else to care for Mom. His sadness about his lost brother. His confusion over what to do about Hayley and their pretend relationship and the kiss they'd shared.

And most of all, his own feelings about her.

Every time he was close to her, he wanted more.

He wanted forever. Wanted to live with her in sickness and health, for richer or poorer, for the rest of their lives, like his parents. Wanted to raise children with her. Wanted to see that sunny smile and hear that throaty chuckle every single day.

It wasn't going to happen. Couldn't. The reason was crystal-clear today of all days, when his brother was at the forefront of his mind. If not for Nate's negligence, Tom would still be alive. He'd be here laughing and teasing and celebrating the day.

Nate didn't deserve a good woman. Not only that, but he didn't know how to handle things with Hayley, given the secret he knew about her past and her biological child.

It couldn't happen, but that didn't stop the wanting.

He should never have kissed her, but at the same time, he couldn't regret it. It had been the best kiss, the best moment, of his life.

He paused at the stream, waiting for his father to catch up, ready to offer a hand if he slipped on the steep, rocky ground. Dad was strong, but Mom's illness had aged him. How old was he now…sixty-five? Old enough to wince when he got into or out of a kneeling position.

The sun shone hot on Nate's back, and the water ran sparkling clear at his feet. Cold, when he reached down to rinse his hand after baiting his hook. He and his father weren't fancy fly fishermen; they fished with live bait, for food. At this time of year, they didn't use waders, either, but wore old sneakers. Working class fishing, Dad called it, and it was the only kind Nate knew.

He watched Dad cast his line out into the stream, his movement easy and assured, the result of many years of practice. He reeled in his line slowly. Then more slowly, then he stopped.

The tip of his fishing pole wasn't moving, so it wasn't that he had a fish on. When Nate looked at his face, it was set in careworn lines, and his gaze had settled on the ponderosa pines on the ridge above.

"You okay, Dad?"

"Oh, fine." Dad started reeling in his line again.

"Are you really?" Nate set his own line drifting so he could focus on his father.

Dad reeled in his line the rest of the way and then cast again before answering. "I'm worried about your mother, just like all of us."

Nate nodded. "It's tough. As a pastor, I'm supposed to have words at the ready, but when it's my own family... I just don't."

Dad didn't look at him. "Not sure how I'm

going to do this life without her." His voice choked up a little at the end.

His father would be mortified for Nate to see him cry, so Nate said, "I know," patted Dad's arm, and then focused his attention on his own fishing and on settling his own emotions. He didn't know how to do life without his mother, either.

Eventually, he pulled in a brook trout and, when he looked over, Dad was smiling. "Good job. Now we need about ten of those, or maybe a few rainbows."

"Hey, I did my part, it's your turn," he joked.

"Can't you see I'm sending all the big fish your way?" Then his face went serious. "I've been blessed. It's a wonderful love your mother and I have, and it's been a wonderful marriage."

"I know." Now it was Nate's voice that was choking up.

"I want the same for you." Dad cast again.

Nate pulled in an empty hook and baited it. "We're not talking about me, we're talking about you."

"I wonder," Dad said, "if we never talked about you enough. Tom was always out there, always needing something, getting into trouble. You were the easy twin. You're still trying to be perfect, but you don't have to be."

"Thanks. I... I appreciate that, but you didn't

do anything wrong." Determined to get the focus off himself and the uncomfortable truths Dad was revealing, he said, "When something... something happens, to Mom, you know we'll always be here for you."

"I know." But his father's face remained sad. He didn't say what he was surely thinking: having kids wasn't the same as having a wife, a life partner.

His parents had had a love for the ages, and Nate wanted the same thing for himself, and he wasn't going to have it. That was a loss and a regret he'd always carry.

"Son," Dad said, "this is the last thing I'm going to say about it. I'm sorry we allowed it to be all about your brother. We'll do better next... next year." His voice had gone low at the last words, and Nate could easily figure out why.

Dad was wondering whether Mom would be there next year.

They fished a little longer, focused on it and pulled in several more brookies and four beautiful rainbow trout, two each. It was plenty for dinner, and it was a joyous experience to be fishing together. Mom was wise; she'd known what they'd both needed.

As they went to the car, the sun dipped behind the mountain peak, throwing the valley into a premature dusk. A Steller's jay cawed from a branch above him, answered by its mate in an adjoining tree.

Nate put an arm around his father. "Good trip. Thanks."

"We should do it more," Dad said in a sort of growl.

"We will." And Nate vowed to make it so.

He'd maybe done something to comfort his father—or maybe not—but his father had focused more on comforting him. That wasn't how it was supposed to be.

Nate vowed to himself that he'd do better, be a better son. Not perfect, like Dad had accused him of trying to be; that wasn't possible, and Nate knew it.

But he'd try to be a better son, better than he'd been as a brother.

Chapter Ten

Hayley went back to the house, riding with one of Nate's sisters and his mother. She sat and visited for a few minutes and then, while Nate's mom lay down, she played with his sister's kids. The older girl, Ava, raced around the yard in her pink motorized car, screeching to a halt just on the verge of hitting Hayley. That, since the child's speed was at most three miles per hour, wasn't scary. The younger one, Brenna, tried to follow along on her bicycle, and she actually *did* run into Hayley, causing her mother to rush out and scold her.

Hayley waved off the concern. "I love playing with them," she said truthfully. "I could hang out here with them for hours."

"Well, Mom's napping and I'm catching up on some work email, so if you're willing, I'll take you up on that. Not hours, but maybe half an hour more."

"Go. They're sweet and I'm glad to spend time with them."

She wasn't just being nice. Spending time around younger children gave Hayley a sharp, joyous pang.

She was getting her teaching degree so that she could teach at Bright Tomorrows, and she knew she was suited to the older aged children, boys in particular. She had a knack with them. But that didn't mean she didn't love smaller kids. Being around these cuties—who were now digging a hole in the dirt, talking about treasure they might find—made her long for children of her own.

Made her long for her own son.

You made the right plan for him. She believed that. She'd been in no shape to be a mother. Although the pregnancy had jolted her into giving up drugs and alcohol for the time being, she hadn't had a job, and she hadn't been hanging around with the right crowd. Certainly, her baby's father had had no interest in taking care of him and couldn't support him.

She could have kept him with her and cared for him, and she knew she would have loved him, but she also knew he would have had a hard life. She'd had no extended family to help, and no confidence that she could find work. She'd feared she might go back to substance abuse again.

Feared she might be as bad a parent as her own parents had been.

Making an adoption plan had been the only way. She'd never prayed as hard as she had during that last trimester, when she'd been trying to decide what to do. Having no long-term, caring friends to rely on at that point in her life, she'd been thrown into relying on the people at the pregnancy support center, and on God.

She'd read so much about adopted children in the Bible. She'd learned that God considered all His people His adopted children. The frequency with which she'd turned to those verses in the Bible had steered her toward the course she'd chosen.

That didn't mean it had been easy, and it didn't mean she'd felt happy about herself for making the choice. Guilt and regret were feelings she'd lived with daily since handing her child over to the social worker.

She didn't even know his name. She'd felt that naming was a privilege reserved for the person who would actually raise him.

Hayley shook off the memories and focused on the two adorable kids in front of her, helping them finish digging their hole. When no treasure appeared, she suggested that they choose a selection of shiny rocks to bury for someone else to find.

They did that with the same vigor as they'd searched for treasure, focused fully on the moment.

That was what she needed to do. There was a lot to be learned from children.

After they'd all gone inside, Nate's mother came back into the kitchen, looking more rested. She pulled out a bag of potatoes and started to peel them. That made Hayley smack her forehead. "I forgot. I was planning to spend the afternoon making food for a couple of friends."

Mrs. Fisher laughed. "It's your day off! You shouldn't be cooking."

"I love it," Hayley said. "It's fun to make food on a smaller scale rather than for a big group of ravenous boys. Plus, I want to help out my friends."

"What are you making?"

"A couple of breakfast casseroles. You know, the ones with potatoes and sausage and eggs? For my friend Emily, since she and her husband have new foster kids who just arrived. This will get their days off to a good start."

"I know them," Mrs. Fisher said. "That's a kind gesture."

Hayley sat down at the table and pulled out her

phone to tap in a list. "Then I'm doing one for Ashley—do you know her and Jason?"

"A little. From church."

"His mother isn't well, and I know they're spending tons of time on the road, back and forth to Denver. Plus, Ashley's pregnant. She doesn't need to spend her time cooking." She tapped her fingers on the table. "I'll put vegetables in Ashley's, since she's health conscious. For Emily and Dev and the kids, I'll leave them out. Veggies don't always go over well with kids."

"Cook it here," Nate's mom suggested. "I'd love the company."

"You're so sweet. But I doubt you have all the ingredients here, and I wouldn't want to—"

"You don't understand," Mrs. Fisher said. "Dan loves to shop at warehouse stores. Plus, he grew up poor and likes to have things stockpiled. Believe me, we could open a grocery store here."

"Well…" It *would* be nice to stay. Easier than stopping at the grocery store and then going home to bake. Not to mention bothering someone for a ride. She pulled up the recipe on her phone and Mrs. Fisher looked at it and nodded. "Eggs, check. Cheese. We have hot and mild sausage. You'll have to use real potatoes and make the dough, but I'm guessing that's not hard for you to do."

"Nope, I would do that anyway. And I'll send

Nate over with replacements for everything I use."

"Don't worry about that." Mrs. Fisher grasped her hand. "I'm just glad you can stay."

Suddenly, Hayley was glad she was staying, too. She wanted to spend more time with this woman and she liked making her happy. "Tell me where I can grab stuff, and I'll get started. I'll make a casserole for you all, too, to have tomorrow."

"That would be lovely."

So, Hayley grated potatoes and put together dough while Mrs. Fisher made a salad and rice to go with the fish they were hoping the men would bring home.

"What was Nate like as a child?" Hayley asked as she mixed up flour and baking powder and salt. "Was he always a good boy?"

Mrs. Fisher burst out laughing. "Not by a long shot. He and his brother climbed a dresser and got into their father's shaving supplies when they were barely a year old. They'd egg each other on, see, and help each other." She smiled fondly. "Dan and I were a little older when we had the twins, and I suppose we weren't as tight with the discipline as we were with their big sisters. At any rate, both of them got into their share of scrapes, especially Tom."

Her face went sad for a moment and then she

turned from the tomato she was chopping and pointed a knife at Hayley. "You're good at asking questions, but Dan and I realized lately that we don't know as much about you. Are your parents nearby?"

Hayley frowned. "That's a good question. We're in touch sporadically, and it's been a while."

Mrs. Fisher looked surprised. Obviously, her own children knew where she and her husband were at all times. Hayley waved a hand around the kitchen. "My family isn't like this," she said, and explained about her parents and her grandmother.

Mrs. Fisher moved closer and palmed Hayley's back. "I'm sorry, dear. That sounds hard to deal with."

"It was, I guess, though it was all I knew," Hayley said. "I've really been enjoying being a part of your family."

"We love having you here, and seeing you and Nate," Mrs. Fisher said. She hesitated. "Is it okay if I ask you a personal question?"

Hayley froze. "Okay," she said cautiously.

"Do you want to have children?"

Hayley's insides clamped together and she felt like crying. She *did* want to have children, of course, but she'd resigned herself to not doing it. But wouldn't it be amazing if she could actually have kids, a family? "If I did," she said, "I'd want a family like yours."

"That's very sweet," she said. "I just wondered because…well, I think Nate would be such a good father."

The back door opened and Nate came in. He looked from one to the other. "What did I miss?"

"We were just talking about children and what a good father you'd be," his mother said smoothly.

Nate's eyebrows lifted as he looked at Hayley. "That's a little premature, Mom," he said. "Let's focus on one thing at a time. Hayley and I are still getting to know each other."

Thank you, Hayley mouthed to Nate. She busied herself sprinkling cheese on her casserole dishes.

At the same time, some aching, longing part of her wished he hadn't been quite so quick to dismiss the idea.

Mrs. Fisher smiled. "I guess the bigger question is, did you bring home enough fish, or are we going to have to eat Hayley's breakfast casseroles for dinner?"

"Oh ye of little faith." Nate's father came in carrying a cooler. "Four nice rainbows and six brookies. We could feed an army."

Hayley took deep breaths and tried to loosen her shoulders. Nate's mom hadn't meant anything by asking about children, hadn't known it would pain Hayley.

But what they were doing, deceiving this lovely family, had lots of potential to cause pain.

Hayley needed to think long and hard about that, and maybe talk to Nate about the possibility of changing course.

Nate had every intention of taking Hayley home quickly and then going home himself. Dinner had been loaded with all kinds of insinuations. "So, Hayley, you like to cook family-sized meals as well as for a crowd" and "It's great how much you love children" and finally, "Nate, she's a keeper."

It had been awkward, and the only saving grace had been the happy expression on his mother's face.

Of course, he'd had to show Hayley some affection, taking her hand and putting an arm around her. Far from being a hardship, it had been a pleasure. Too much of one. He'd liked being close to her way too much, had found himself pretending it could be real, could last forever.

That was why he needed to get away from her pronto. But instead, here he was sitting with her on Ashley and Jason's porch.

They'd already dropped off one casserole at Emily and Dev's newly chaotic home, had met the foster kids, praised Landon for how well he was doing as a new brother, and offered encouragement to Emily and Dev, who'd both looked shell-shocked but happy.

Ashley and Jason had been going out the door, headed down to Denver to check on Jason's mother, when Nate and Hayley had arrived with the food Hayley had made.

"Stay, enjoy the porch," Ashley said. "We get a great view of the sunset. And thanks for this." She took hold of the cooler containing the breakfast casserole. "We'll take it along and, this way, we won't have to grocery shop or cook right away."

Nate knew they shouldn't stay, but he couldn't make himself say it. It seemed like it would be mean to Hayley after she'd spent the day sacrificing her time and energy for his family. He waited for her to suggest leaving—surely she would—but after she hugged Ashley and Jason, and their truck's taillights disappeared, she came back onto the porch and settled into a rocking chair.

He sucked in a breath, let out a sigh and tried not to notice the way the golden light kissed Hayley's hair.

He had to do something to get his emotions in check, so he put on his pastor's hat. "I can tell you're a strong woman of faith now," he said, "but the other night—" He broke off, stricken. The other night, the night they'd *kissed*... He cleared his throat and pushed past the awkward feeling. "The other night, you talked about being into drugs and running with the wrong people. What happened to turn that around?"

She looked at him, assessing, then wrinkled her nose and looked away. It was as if she didn't think he really wanted to, or should, hear that story.

"It's not my business," he said quickly. "We can talk about something else. Or not talk."

She looked at him then. "I'm not sure it's something you want to hear."

Oh. She was going to tell him about her baby. And, against his better judgment, he *did* want to hear the story. "I'm a pastor," he said. "I've heard it all. And I care about you—"

"Nate."

"As a friend," he added quickly. "But it's your call."

The sun was sinking behind the mountains, tinting the few puffy clouds with gold. Birds trilled and peeped, seeming to want to share one last song.

Hayley was quiet for several minutes. Just as he thought she wasn't going to speak, she looked over at him. "Among that wrong crowd I was running with, there was this guy."

He slowed his breathing, nodded. He kind of didn't want to hear it, kind of did. He definitely didn't want her to feel judged. "Go on."

"It's not an uncommon story," she said. "We were at a friend's apartment, late at night. Everyone else had gone to bed. I guess he…he thought I was like some of the other girls, not caring who I slept with. I wasn't, but I was too high and drunk to make that clear."

He reached out and took her hand as gently as he could. "Did he assault you?"

"No. No, not really. I just… I guess I figured, oh well, it was bound to happen sometime. I didn't try to stop him." She swallowed hard. "When he realized it was my first time, he just left. I mean…" She cleared her throat. "Right afterward."

Nate's clasp stiffened. Inside, he wanted to beat the tar out of that guy, but he needed to stay calm for Hayley. "I'm sorry. That stinks."

"Yeah. I was pretty upset." She cleared her throat and pulled her hand away from his. "Especially when I realized I was pregnant."

"Wow." Nate blew out a breath. So that was how it had happened.

"I went to him and told him. He called me a liar, said it couldn't happen the first time."

"What did you do?"

She shrugged. "I had no one. No one who

could deal with that big of an issue. Not that a pregnancy is just an issue, it's a baby, but…" She lifted her hands, palms up. "It was hard. I felt so alone. Finally, a friend told me about this crisis pregnancy center, and I went there, and they helped me." Her eyes shone with unshed tears. "They were wonderful. They helped me find cheap, safe housing, and a part-time job."

"I thank God for places like that."

"Yeah. I donate part of every paycheck to them. Anyway, they also had counseling, and they encouraged me to go to church, and the people there were kind, too. I figured out what I'd been missing." She gave him a brief, watery smile. "A long answer to your question."

"I'm glad you told me. And I'm glad you got help and support."

She nodded. "Aren't you going to ask what happened to the baby?"

Nate's heart started pounding. Was this the moment he should tell her what he knew…what Stan had told him?

But that was confidential. And in this moment, it might serve Hayley better to just be able to talk it through. "Tell me," he said.

"It was a boy. I nursed him for two days, for the nutrients he could get. And then I…" Her voice quivered and she stopped.

He scooted his chair closer so that he could put

an arm around her. "It's okay. You don't have to talk about it."

"Might as well finish the story," she said with a high little laugh. "I placed him for adoption. Or rather, had him placed through an agency."

"That took so much courage."

She leaned forward until she was bent double, hands over her face. "It was awful," she choked out, "I miss him every day."

"Oh, Hayley." He knelt beside her and put his arms around her, and as the sky turned a deep purple, he held her as she cried.

His heart burned with compassion for her, for what she'd been through. At the same time, his mind raced with his double knowledge.

He knew, now, what had happened to cause Hayley to place her baby for adoption. Unbeknownst to her, he also knew who that baby was and where he was. Tomorrow, when they went back to work, they'd be with Jeremy every day.

It was impossible to tell her that. Impossible, too, not to tell her.

Impossible not to feel incredibly close to her after what she'd revealed.

He let his head rest against her back, his arms around her, and tried to figure out what to do.

Chapter Eleven

It was the day of the big field trip to the dinosaur fossil grounds. Hayley was excited, but also wary.

For one thing, several board members had said they might stop by the site, including the difficult Arlene. Stan would also be there for part of the day, as he was heading off to see a specialist in Denver. He'd desperately wanted to join this field trip because he'd planned it.

The other thing that was making her extremely nervous was yesterday. All of it had been emotionally intense. She'd realized how much she cared for Nate's family. She'd felt for them in their pain about Nate's brother and about Mrs. Fisher's illness.

But last night…wow. She'd spilled all the garbage from her past on Nate. And rather than judging her or turning away, he'd listened and held her.

He was so kind and so good. He embodied everything she would have wanted in a man, if she'd felt that she deserved a man.

She didn't. But a tiny sliver of light had shone into the dark areas of her heart last night.

Nate hadn't condemned her. He'd heard about the worst mistake of her life and he hadn't rejected her for it.

The bus bumped and jostled down the last dirt road and finally pulled into the dinosaur monument. It was a branch of one of the bigger fossil preserves, but it featured a small museum and a couple of areas where the public could make arrangements to come in and dig for fossils.

They got out, and summer heat hit as if an oven door had been opened. "Man, this stinks," groused one of the boys.

Another let out a swear word, quickly muffled, which Hayley chose to ignore. "We're not in the mountains anymore," she said. "This will make us appreciate how cool we usually have it at Bright Tomorrows."

Stan and Arlene arrived in a luxury BMW sedan that Hayley knew didn't belong to the math teacher. Sure enough, Arlene got out, grumbling about the dust and the bumpy road, and what it might have done to her vehicle.

"Now, Arlene, you wouldn't expect an active archaeological site on a well traveled main road,"

Stan said. He rubbed his hands together. "This is going to be great."

Stan's enthusiasm brightened Hayley's mood. "I'm so glad you could come," she said to Stan. "This was a great idea."

Arlene snorted under her breath.

The boys were milling around, some gravitating toward the fence that protected the dig site, others toward the museum, which Hayley hoped was air-conditioned.

Nate flashed a smile at her and followed the latter group of boys.

Hayley's stomach flipped as she watched him go. When she'd gotten on the bus, he'd already boarded and was in the back, and she'd deliberately sat in front. She didn't want him to think that, just because she'd been a total dishrag last night, he was obligated to take care of her this morning, or act as her best friend.

His smile just now told her he wasn't holding last night against her, and joy sparked from her head to her toes.

Maybe this can work.

Stan came up beside her. "Let's put an emphasis on how there are career opportunities in fields like this if the boys are interested," he said.

He'd already sent her an email about this very subject, and it had been in the camp publicity, too, but she didn't complain. "Will do. Maybe you could talk to some of the boys about it as well."

"I'll do that. I'm just here for the first half of the day, but I intend to make the most of it."

A uniformed park employee had come out and was talking to Nate. They seemed to agree on something, because the man beckoned to the boys by the fence. "If you could all come inside, we'll watch a short film before putting you to work on the dig," he said.

They all trooped inside, cheered considerably by the air conditioning and the big tray of doughnuts set out for them.

Nate sat at the back of the room and, when Hayley glanced over, he patted the chair beside him. Her heart rate accelerated and her palms got sweaty.

This isn't a date! It's a science talk for teens!

Her self-scolding didn't slow down her breathing one whit. She sat beside him, grateful the room wasn't bright.

The ranger spoke for a few minutes, welcoming the boys and joking with them, clearly at ease and capturing their attention, which let Hayley and Nate off the hook for discipline duties. Even the counselors seemed engaged. Reggie, who was becoming Hayley's favorite, looked over and gave them a thumbs-up.

Jeremy, Snowflake at his side, was seated beside his mother, looking less than thrilled. She must have insisted he sit with her, and now, she raised her hand. "Jeremy has been interested in dinosaurs since he was a little tyke," she said proudly. "He used to be able to name more than a hundred species."

Jeremy's face flamed red. The poor kid. Didn't Arlene know that boys didn't like to be singled out, especially for an obscure interest like dinosaurs?

Fortunately, the speaker took it in stride. "We may call you to report out on them," he said easily, "but these days, we're finding that the number of dinosaur species is actually in flux. New fossils are being discovered all the time. Maybe some of you will discover one today! And dinos we thought were new species are actually part of another group. Did you know we've found a teenage T-Rex?"

He went on, keeping the boys' interest. Stan said something to Arlene, and she then whispered to Jeremy and both of the adults moved to another seat in the back, leaving Jeremy to move down and sit with the other boys. Good on Stan.

Snowflake moved beside him, still panting, and Hayley noticed that Jeremy kept his hand on her.

"This was a great idea," Nate said, keeping his voice low so as not to disturb the speaker.

"It was, and I can't take credit. Stan wants to stoke their interest in STEM careers. If it's a hit, they may do more science-related field trips like this during the school year."

Soon, the ranger led them all outside.

"Hey, look!" Booker pointed to the sky.

A hot-air balloon was floating overhead. Hayley clapped her hands and stopped beside Booker to watch it. "So pretty."

"None of those back home." Booker stared upward then turned 360 degrees to survey the area. "Man, I love it here! Wish I could live in Colorado." He gave Hayley a spontaneous hug and then backed away quickly, his skin darkening with a blush. He looked around quickly as if hoping none of the other boys had seen.

They hadn't, so Hayley put an arm around him and gave him a quick squeeze. "I'm glad you're here." Moments like these, she knew teaching was the right career for her. She loved these kids and she loved making a difference in their lives.

The ranger called the boys down to a sandbox-type structure to show them how to dig without damaging anything. Hayley and Nate followed, more slowly.

It was now or never. "Look, I'm sorry about last night," she said. "I lost it, and you were so kind, but it won't happen again."

"It's okay if it does," he said, his voice a low rumble. "I liked being close to you."

She glanced over at him quickly and their eyes met. Held.

Suddenly, it was a little bit hard to breathe.

A throat cleared behind them. Stan. Hayley jumped away from Nate as if she'd been caught doing something wrong. "I'd better go on down and see what the boys are learning," she said breathlessly.

"I'll be right there," Nate said. "Stan, a moment?"

The two men walked off to the side and Hayley went toward the boys, her face burning. She needed to keep her distance from Nate, especially with Stan and Arlene here. She had to get that good recommendation from Stan and from a board member. Nothing could interfere with that.

After the brief lesson, the ranger led the boys over to the fossil field. Soon they were spread out and digging away, with the ranger circulating to make sure everyone was following instructions and being careful.

The sun baked down, even though it was barely 10:00 a.m. The ground was dusty and dry, and a smell of sagebrush perfumed the air.

Jeremy chose a spot near a small resource hut, but a couple of the other boys objected. "That's the only shady spot on the field," Mickey complained.

"Snowflake needs the shade," he said, and indeed, the fluffy dog plopped down beside him, panting.

"Is she okay?" Hayley walked over. She hadn't considered how hot it would be down here in the valley and how hard that might be on a dog bred for icier climates.

"I *think* so," Jeremy said. He looked over to his mom, then at Snowflake.

"Do you want me to ask your mom if she should stay outside in this heat?" Hayley offered quietly once the other boys had settled into their digging and weren't in listening distance.

"Yeah. I don't want anything to happen to her."

"I'll ask your mom what she thinks. And I'll get a bowl of water for Snowflake."

Jeremy looked stricken. "I forgot."

"It's okay." Hayley reflected on what a lot of responsibility an animal was for a boy. Jeremy was fairly mature for thirteen, but he was still a child.

"Remember," the ranger was telling the boys as Hayley walked away, "if you find a fossil, it may be a turtle, a crocodile or a fish, because Colorado was mostly under water at the time this layer of rock was at the surface."

Arlene was inside the building, so, after Hayley had filled a water dish for Snowflake, she went over to the woman. "Is it okay for Snowflake to be outside in this heat? Jeremy wanted me to ask you, although I don't think he wanted to call attention to needing something from his mom in front of the other boys."

"Some time outside is fine," Arlene said. "In half an hour, he can bring her inside to sit with me."

"Sounds good."

Arlene walked outside with her, and they found all the boys clustered around Booker, who was hovering over a small bone. "Looks like the tailbone of a something in the *fruitadens* family," the ranger said. "Good job." He smiled at Booker, and the boy glowed.

All of the campers went back to digging with renewed vigor. Hayley took the bowl of water to Snowflake, who still lay in the shade. Mickey had come over and was digging beside Jeremy.

She watched for a moment and then backed off to give them their space. She soon found herself standing beside Nate.

"It's great to see this," she said. "I think we'll do a program on scientific careers, maybe a movie, if I can find one. Do you think that's a good idea?"

"I do," he said. "I almost always like your ideas." He smiled at her and she felt her face flame. There was no reason for it, but she still felt embarrassed.

Or maybe there *was* a reason for it, because it seemed like his gaze flickered to her lips.

Did he want to kiss her again? Did she want him to?

"Hey, there's a fossil!" Mickey and Jeremy both grabbed for a bone, something they had been told not to do.

"I found it!"

"No, I found it!"

There was a sharp crack and both boys dropped the now-broken bone, looking horrified.

"You broke it!"

"No, you broke it!"

Arlene marched toward the two boys. "What's going on?"

The ranger hurried over, along with Reggie, the nearest counselor. "Okay, men, this is why we're careful with the bones." He knelt to study the bone. Then he looked up at them and gave a wry grin. "And this is why it's best to have everyone dig in their own area. I've seen adult men do the exact same thing you two just did."

"Which doesn't make it right," Reggie added.

"I'm really sorry," Jeremy said, looking miserable. "You can have the shady spot, Mick. Mom, can you take Snowflake inside?"

"I can." She turned to Hayley. "And then I'd

like to talk to you inside. You, too," she added, looking at Nate.

Uh-oh. Arlene had seemed friendly when Hayley had spoken with her about Snowflake, but now she was back to being critical. Hayley had no clue what she'd done to change the woman's attitude.

If only she didn't care. If only she could let it roll off her.

But Arlene clearly had Stan's ear, and probably influenced the board as well. Hayley needed positive letters of recommendation from both to do the teaching program.

She looked up at the clear blue sky, then down at the field of fossils. God had created both on His infinite timeline. She needed to remember that her own problems were a grain of sand by comparison, and the outcome was in God's hands.

She shot up a prayer for perspective and then waited to make sure that all the boys were settled in again. The ranger was talking to Jeremy in a reassuring way, and the boy looked a little more cheerful. Good. Jeremy was smart, and interested in science, and having him make a positive association with this work was important. Mickey stood next to Jeremy, listening to the ranger, their dispute apparently resolved.

"I'm heading in," Nate called to Hayley, giving her an encouraging smile, and after another check of the area, she followed.

Arlene was sitting in a comfortable chair and Stan in another, leaving Nate and Hayley with no place to sit. Stan started to stand, but Hayley waved him back. "No, you sit. You're the convalescent."

Nate glanced around the room. "I'll get us a couple of folding chairs."

Once they were all seated, Arlene looked at Hayley severely then at Nate. "That mishap wouldn't have happened if the two of you had been paying attention," she said. "You were making eyes at one another and an important fossil was broken as a result."

"Now, honey," Stan said, "it's not as if the boys destroyed something important. The ranger said that particular bone was from a crow and was recent. No harm done."

"Maybe, but Jeremy was upset. And the point remains." She glared at Nate and Hayley again. "You two need to concentrate on the boys, not each other."

Hayley bit her lip. "I'm sorry if it seemed like we weren't paying attention…" she started.

"I know you two are involved, but you need to keep that out of the workday. It's inappropriate."

Both Nate and Stan spoke at once.

"We're *friends*," Nate said.

"I haven't seen anything inappropriate," Stan added.

Hayley felt chilled in the air-conditioning. She knew she needed to back away from Nate. Now her connection with him was jeopardizing her ability to get her recommendation and become a teacher. That was all-important. More important than anything.

Anything?

The nagging voice in her head stopped Hayley still as the others went on talking about other things.

For the past year and a half, she'd been focused on getting her degree and becoming a teacher. That was supposed to make up for what she couldn't have, the love of a good man, children.

But maybe love was more important. Maybe she *could* have that.

Was it possible she could have both?

She didn't deserve it. But there was that light, shining into her darkness, the door opening a little wider. Maybe the past *could* be forgiven. Someday.

Soon it was time to round up the boys for lunch, which they'd brought in brown paper bags. They gathered in the auditorium to eat, the smell of peanut butter and the sound of excited boys filling the air.

Arlene and Stan left for his doctor's appoint-

ment, Arlene hugging Jeremy and frowning at
Hayley and Nate, Stan giving both of them a
thumbs-up.

"Let's sit together on the bus," Nate suggested
as they started their afternoon activities. "We
can talk."

She wanted to, but knew it wasn't wise. "That's
just what we can't do," she said. "We're giving
people the wrong impression."

"Later, then," he said. "I think we've created
enough controversy that we need to hash it out."

"You're right, we do," Hayley said. "But in
private." That sounded like she was suggesting
more than a talk, and her face heated. "Somewhere neutral. Not our houses."

"I have work to catch up on at the church, once
we get back," Nate said. "Why don't you come
to my office?"

"Sounds good." But as they figured out a time,
Hayley wondered, would hashing it out lead to
more togetherness, or an end to what togetherness they had?

In his office that evening, Nate surveyed the
numerous emails in need of answers, the notes
from the part-time church secretary, and the
stack of books and papers that represented his
as-yet-unplanned sermon.

So much to do, and yet all that was on his mind was Hayley.

He'd loved being with her today, seeing her excitement about the fossils, watching her skill with the boys, noticing the way the sunshine turned her hair golden. She was more and more at the forefront of his mind.

She was coming to his office in just half an hour.

He'd pulled Stan aside this afternoon to discuss the possibility of telling Hayley the truth about Jeremy. Even though he'd laid out all the reasons it would be a good idea, and pointed out the risks of keeping such a secret, Stan had been emphatic. Nate *couldn't* tell Hayley. He'd promised. The truth would be too damaging to Arlene, who was in a bad place right now, and possibly to Jeremy.

Nate had argued but Stan had held firm and, finally, Nate had agreed to keep the confidence. What choice had he had? The best he'd been able to do was to warn Stan that he would revisit the issue at a later date.

Stan had insisted he wouldn't change his mind, that letting the secret out would be a disaster.

The older man's vehemence had cemented Nate's dilemma.

He couldn't tell Hayley the truth. That meant

he couldn't get too close with her. The trouble was, his heart wanted closeness, and a lot of it.

Rather than sitting down and starting to answer emails, he turned to the small altar in the back corner of his office and sank to his knees.

The church was empty and, for a few minutes, he just listened to the silence and cleared his mind.

Then, as always, he started his prayers with his family. Meditating on his brother, now in Heaven. Asking that Mom's illness be cured or that she would continue to be given the strength and faith to handle what came. His father, his sisters, his nieces and nephews.

Hayley. His prayed for her to find peace of mind, well-being and strength. Prayed that she achieve the goal she'd set for herself, that of becoming a teacher.

Prayed for the two of them, that they settle into the right type of relationship, whatever the Lord's will.

A soft ringing sound indicated that someone had come into the church, so he offered his final thanks and rose to his feet. A few seconds later, there was a quiet tapping on his door.

"Come in," he said. His heart pounded like a marching band's bass drum.

She'd changed into a casual dress and her hair hung loose around her shoulders. Accustomed to seeing Hayley in shorts and T-shirts, hair in a ponytail, he was tongue-tied to see how pretty she looked.

Had she cleaned up and dressed up for him? His mouth went dry at the thought.

"Hi," she said, her voice hesitant. "Is this still an okay time?"

"Yes, of course, come in. Have a seat." He wanted to hug her, but he knew better than to go in that direction. "All recovered from today?"

She sank gracefully into the chair on the opposite side of his desk. "I'm a little tired," she admitted.

"Me, too." Nate didn't like sitting behind a desk to talk to people, so he came out from behind it and sat in the chair catty-corner from her. "It was a good trip, though. I think the boys really enjoyed it. Did they settle down?"

She nodded. "The counselors had a brilliant idea. They're showing *Jurassic Park* on the outdoor screen."

Nate laughed. "That's perfect."

They looked at each other steadily for a moment and then both started to speak at once.

"We need to figure out—" he began.

"What are we going to do about—" she said.

They both laughed, awkwardly. "You first," he said.

"Okay. We need to figure out what to do

about…well, about how our relationship is perceived," she said. "Stan and Arlene seem to think we're involved."

He started to say *We are*, and then didn't. He needed to let her speak her piece and to see where she stood.

"We're not," she said, directly contradicting what Nate thought, "but we're pretending to be, to your family."

"It's a bit of a mess, isn't it?" Honesty compelled him to add, "My feelings have gotten involved, too."

Her cheeks went pink. "Because we kissed."

"Well," he said slowly, "I wanted to kiss you because my feelings have gotten involved. On my side, at least, the feelings came first."

"Mine, too," she said quietly and then stared at her knees. "But it can't happen."

Her words made his heart plummet, but he cleared his throat and kept going, doggedly, "You want to focus on your goal to become a teacher," he said. "Right?"

"Ye-e-es," she said slowly. "And also…"

"What?"

She bit her lip and then met his eyes. "You're a pastor, Nate. A good man, who deserves a good woman. That's not me."

"Whoa, whoa, whoa." He leaned forward and reached out to take her hand, then stopped himself. Touching Hayley was dangerous. "You're a good person, Hayley. You're kind, and caring, and you pretty much devote your life to helping others."

"Thanks." Now she was looking at him steadily. "But you know what I mean."

"I don't."

She blew out a sigh. "You're going to make me say it, aren't you? I had a *baby*, Nate. And rather than take care of him, I gave him up. I was hooked on drugs and alcohol. That's a whole world of not-goodness."

He opened his mouth to protest.

She waved a hand, silencing him. "You deserve a woman without that kind of a past. A pastor's wife who can be a good example to other women. Not someone people talk about."

He studied her troubled face. "You know you're forgiven by God for mistakes you made in the past, right? That's what Christ did for us. He took on our sins."

"I *know* it," she said, "but I don't *know* it. If that makes sense."

"You haven't taken it in."

"Right." She sighed. "It's something I have to work on, but in the meantime, yes, I'm focused on my goal of becoming a teacher. I can't be doing things that are going to make me look bad in front of people like Stan. Nate, I need him to write me a strong recommendation, and I need his help to get a board recommendation. Arlene's, too, most likely. Otherwise, I won't be able to start that fast-track teaching program in the fall."

"Okay." It was disappointing, but it made sense and, on a deep level, Nate could identify. "I want to make the camp a success, too. And you're right, we can't do anything that might jeopardize it. It's too important for the boys."

She nodded, looking relieved. And then she studied him. "I know why I'm dedicated," she said, "but why are you?"

Maybe it was the evening, or the day they'd had, that pushed him to dig deep and be honest. "I feel like I have to do twice as much."

"Because...?" She waited.

He shrugged. "My brother."

"Ohhhh." She frowned. "Is that really logical? He died, so you have to take on his life burden yourself?"

"He could have done so much if I had stopped him from going to war."

"Nate." She leaned forward and touched his hand. "Really? You blame yourself for not stopping him? When, actually, it sounds like you only joined up because of him?"

When she put it like that, it sounded kind of ridiculous. It also made him feel defensive. "You didn't know him. He was wild, a hothead.

I was the calm, reasonable twin, and I stopped him from getting into a lot of trouble. Just not enough."

"You didn't stop him from enlisting."

"Right."

"So you're to blame for his death and you have to live your life doing twice the work to make up for it?"

"It's not—"

"Did you ever talk to your sisters about this?" she interrupted.

The question surprised him. "No. Why would I?"

"Because maybe they feel similar," she said, "or maybe they'd have another insight into your family and your brother."

"They weren't as close to him as I was. They were older. I was the one who..." Suddenly, he was flooded with memories. Of him and Tom running through the woods, camping out at the quarry, fishing with their dad. He'd never been alone as a young boy; he'd always had Tom.

His chest felt hollow and he didn't trust himself to speak.

She took his hand in hers, gently. "Look, I'm no counselor. But I wonder if, by doing all this extra work, you're trying to avoid the pain of his loss?"

He looked into her thoughtful eyes and pulled his hand away. "No that's not it."

She shrugged. "Okay. It was just a thought."

"Thanks," he said. He had a feeling he'd come back to her idea and ponder it, especially since she wasn't pushing him to agree with her. For now, though, he wanted to put the past aside and focus on the present. Focus on Hayley.

He leaned forward and grasped both of her hands this time. "It would be nice to explore these feelings," he said. "Figure out if it's just… well, temporary attraction, or something more."

She nodded without looking at him.

"But that would jeopardize your goals," he said. *Plus, I know a huge secret about you.*

An image of the three of them together popped into his mind. Hayley, Jeremy and Arlene. So interconnected, and no one knew about it except him and Stan.

Knowing it and not telling her made him feel like a jerk.

"I feel like a jerk," she said, uncannily echoing his thoughts, "for fooling your family."

"Me, too," he said. "It was a bad idea. Unless…"

Their eyes met. He was still holding her hands. *Unless it's real.*

She pulled her hands away and stood. "I should

go," she said. "Can we just agree to keep a little more distance?"

"Around the boys?"

"Around everyone," she said. She sounded a little choked.

He wanted to pull her into his arms, but she whirled around and went out the door. He heard her sandals click rapidly down the hall.

He blew out a sigh and looked heavenward. This was out of his area of expertise. He had no idea what to do.

But she'd suggested something, and since it was his only idea, he decided to do it. He'd talk to his family, see if they had any insight into the past and his brother.

Meanwhile, he'd try to keep more distance between them. Which wouldn't be easy to do.

Chapter Twelve

The day after the field trip was that rare thing in Colorado: an all-day rain. Fortunately, Hayley had looked at the forecast and called in a favor. Jason, Ashley's husband, was the industrial arts teacher during the school year, and he'd agreed to spend the afternoon working with the boys, teaching them to make a simple birdhouse in the school's woodshop. The activity was optional—the boys were also permitted to take the afternoon as free time—but most had chosen to participate.

Hayley checked in to make sure it was all going well. Boys were measuring wood and drilling holes and taking turns with a circular saw, closely supervised by Jason and a couple of the counselors. Jason's service dog, Titan, lay at ease in the front of the room, clearly off duty. She thanked Jason for stepping in and watched the busy shop for a few minutes, glad the boys seemed to be both learning from and enjoying the project.

As she turned to go, intent on catching up on paperwork and cooking, Jeremy approached her, Snowflake at his side. "Can you help me, Miss Hayley?"

His sweetness disarmed her. "Of course, Jeremy. Come on out into the hall. How can I help?"

"It's Snowflake," he said as he followed her.

"Is something wrong?" Hayley's heart thumped. The dog was panting up at her, all smiles, but that didn't mean she was okay. Jeremy knew her best.

"Look." He knelt and parted a section of the dog's hair, and Hayley immediately saw the problem. Stickers and burrs coated the underside of Snowflake's body.

"Last night after the movie, we went on a night hike, and she got into the weeds," he said.

"Do you know what to do?"

He nodded. "I brush her every day—well, most days—but my mom usually helps me when she needs a bigger groom. Could you…?" He flushed.

He was at that awkward age where he wanted help, but wasn't sure it was right to ask for it. Wanted his mom, but didn't know if that was still okay.

Hayley had so much to get done. But she also knew sometimes a boy needed some one-on-one time and, truth to tell, she loved that, too.

Anyway, if she went off and worked by herself, she knew what she would think about. Nate. Nate. And more Nate.

She needed to put her confused feelings about the man out of her mind and simply be in the moment with a child. "Get your grooming kit and come over to the cafeteria," she told Jeremy. "You can help me get started on some cookies, and then we'll take Snowflake out onto the covered porch and groom her. I'm not the expert, though. You'll have to show me what to do."

"Thanks, Miss Hayley!" His happiness made it all worthwhile. She let Jason know that he wouldn't have Jeremy in class that afternoon and then headed for the cafeteria.

Rain beat against the windows and low clouds obscured the mountains. Her emotions felt as wild and dark as the weather outside.

She shouldn't feel so itchy and churned up, not when she had so much. A wonderful job, good friends, a home in one of the most beautiful places on earth.

It was just that she knew there could have been more. She could have found a better way to handle her teenage angst than drugs and alcohol. Could have placed a higher value on staying chaste until marriage.

Or at least, she could have kept her baby.

Although she questioned that decision on a regular basis, she was pretty sure it had been the right one. An innocent baby shouldn't have to suffer while she figured out how to be a self-supporting, drug-free adult.

She walked into the Bright Tomorrows cafeteria, blowing out a sigh. God worked everything for good. Even though she regretted what she'd done, it had helped her have more empathy for young people who made bad decisions. That was what she'd written on her application for the teaching program: she wanted to work with at-risk kids because she understood their problems from the inside out.

It was a plan that had seemed perfect, and enough, until she'd met Nate. Just the thought of him made heat rise to her face.

He'd said, last night, that he had feelings for her. For *her.*

Her mind couldn't help but create images. She could picture walking down the street with Nate, her hand in his, free to move closer, entitled to be open with her affection. She could imagine a candlelight dinner, looking at each other across the table and letting their gazes linger until they forgot about the food.

She could picture walking down the aisle in a beautiful wedding dress, looking toward the front of the church to where he stood, handsome in a tux, for once not the preacher performing the service, but just a man. The groom.

And, wow, she needed to get those images out of her mind before she melted into a sappy, sentimental puddle right there in the cafeteria.

Fortunately, Jeremy entered the dining hall and headed toward her, Snowflake trotting at his side.

Deliberately, Hayley pushed her romantic thoughts away. She gestured for him to come into the kitchen and showed him the industrial-sized mixer. After he'd washed his hands and settled Snowflake on the mat just outside the kitchen door, she had him measure out flour and sugar and baking powder while she softened butter. They took turns breaking eggs and, after mixing the wet and dry ingredients together and sprinkling in chocolate chips, the dough was ready.

"It looks kind of…plain," Jeremy said.

Hayley lifted an eyebrow. "Should we jazz it up?"

He nodded eagerly. "Mom puts in coconut sometimes, to make the cookies crunchier, but…" He wrinkled his nose. "Yuck."

"We could make them crunchy another way," Hayley said, warming to the idea. She loved getting creative with her cooking. "What about adding in cereal?"

"What kind?" he asked, looking skeptical.

"Let's go look at our options." They walked over to the cereal bins. "Cornflakes would work," Hayley said, "or we could crush up the oat rounds."

"How about chocolate rice crisps?" he suggested. "They're everyone's favorites."

"Done," Hayley said.

"Yeah!"

So they measured out cereal, and Hayley added a little more liquid to compensate for the dryness. "Now the chocolate chips look kind of sparse, though."

Jeremy peeked into the bowl. "Do you have more?"

"Sure, but…what about M&Ms instead?"

"Yeah!" He hugged her spontaneously. "You're a fun cook, Miss Hayley."

Hayley's heart expanded three sizes, just like the Grinch, but she didn't want to gush and embarrass Jeremy. "We'll let the dough chill for a bit while we work on Snowflake," she said. "I think outdoors on the covered porch is best, don't you?"

He laughed. "Yes. Mom hates when I groom her inside, because fur flies everywhere. She has a double coat, don't you, girl?"

Snowflake gave a little half howl, half yip in response.

"She seems to talk to you," Hayley said as they headed to the porch.

"She does." Jeremy ordered Snowflake to lie down and then started opening the grooming kit he'd brought.

When the dog saw the kit, she got to her feet and trotted a few paces away, looking over her shoulder at Jeremy.

"No way, I'm not chasing you." He held out a flat hand. "Touch."

Slowly, Snowflake trudged over and tapped Jeremy's outstretched hand with her nose.

"Good girl. Now, down."

Snowflake locked eyes with the boy for a moment and then plopped down, first her front end, then her back end.

"You're really good with her," Hayley said, impressed.

He smiled, his cheeks going pink. He handed the dog a tiny treat and then ordered her to lie on her side. When she complied, he began brushing her, firmly, lifting up sections of her white coat to get at the fur underneath.

"It can take a long time," he said. "But I don't mind. I like doing it."

Hayley knelt beside him and picked out the burrs as his brushing revealed them. "Did you choose to get a Samoyed, or was she just what was offered?"

"She was offered, but we could've said no," he said as he moved to brush the area of fur over Snowflake's haunch. "Mom thought maybe we should wait for a Lab or a Golden, but as soon as I met Snowflake, I knew she was the dog for me."

"I can tell how much you love each other," Hayley said.

"I do. I had to promise to help with her grooming, and I stuck to it. It's my responsibility."

Snowflake lay quietly on her side, allowing Jeremy to continue brushing her.

Hayley ran in, made a couple big trays of cookies and put them in the oven. Then she returned and took a turn brushing Snowflake before rushing back inside to take out the cookies.

In between, they chatted. Jeremy didn't really seem to need help with the dog brushing, and Hayley realized that what the sensitive boy had really needed was a little time with an adult, a mother figure. She was glad to fulfill that role.

She loved kids, loved helping kids, loved this one-on-one stuff. She wanted that. Yes, she could get a lot of satisfaction out of teaching, but if only she could have children of her own, too... well, that would be the most wonderful thing in the world.

Could she have that with Nate?

Again, she shook off the mental images of what could probably never happen and focused on Jeremy. "Tell me about how you and your mom ended up in Colorado."

"Sure. I was born in Colorado, but after I was adopted, we moved to Indiana. I lived there most of my life until now," he said.

"Wait, you're adopted? I don't think I knew that." There was no reason she should; it wasn't a category on the intake forms.

She wanted desperately to ask him how he felt about being placed for adoption. But it seemed too intrusive.

He answered without her asking. "Sometimes I wonder about my birth mom," he said.

"You're not in touch with her?" Hayley's heart was pounding.

He shook his head. "It was a closed adoption," he said. His expression was a little bit sad.

Hayley felt that to her gut. Was her own son out there somewhere, wondering about her, wishing his adoption hadn't been closed?

Her son would be about Jeremy's age. She looked at him, and a strange feeling washed over her. Could *he* be her son?

She'd had that thought about a few kids over the years, though, and it had always turned out to be wishful thinking. Still, Jeremy's coloring was right, and he'd said he'd been born in Colorado. It was possible…

She wanted to know Jeremy's birth date, but asking him might arouse his suspicions, or worse, his hopes.

She'd never know.

Or, wait…she *could* find out his birth date. It was right in his records.

Tonight, she'd look at the records and see. Even though it would be a ridiculous, huge coincidence, she had to find out the truth. Had to know. Her heart demanded it.

On Friday, after his shift at the camp, Nate decided to head for the church to catch up on the stack of work that awaited him. When he saw the turnoff to his parents' place, though, he impulsively headed in that direction.

There had been something funny in his mother's voice when he'd spoken with her this morning. Something told him to check in.

When he got there, she was pulling out of the driveway, which surprised him. Lately, she hadn't been feeling well enough to drive. He tooted his horn, pulled halfway in and lowered his window. "Where are you headed?"

"To the yarn shop over in Fallsville," she said. "They're open late on Fridays."

Nate squinted. Were her eyes red?

He had way too much to do and zero desire to go to a yarn shop. "Want some company?"

Her face broke into a smile. "I would love that. Could you drive?"

Good. He hadn't wanted to suggest it, but he really didn't want her driving, especially if she was upset. He got out and helped her into the passenger seat of his truck.

Hayley had implied that he should ask his sisters their impressions of how things had been when he and his brother were younger. But his mom was more insightful than anyone else in the family. Maybe this visit, in addition to giving them some good time together, would help him understand the issues that plagued him about his brother.

Maybe it had been a nudge from above that made him come to visit his parents today. And not just to help his mom out, but to get some answers.

They'd no sooner gotten to the end of the street than she spoke up. "There's something on your mind, isn't there?"

He glanced over, raising an eyebrow. "I could say the same to you."

"You go first," she said firmly.

He drove around the corner and headed for the highway. Fallsville was only twenty minutes away, a pretty drive over mountain roads. "I *have* been wondering something," he said.

"Is it related to Hayley?"

He blinked. "How do you know everything?"

"Mothers know." She sounded smug. "What are you wondering about?"

He kept his eyes on the road. "It's really more about Tom," he said. "His decision to enlist. I've always felt guilty that I didn't talk him out of that, and lately it's been making me feel bad about moving on with life."

She stared at him; he could feel it, even though he didn't look over. "Oh, honey, it's not your fault he enlisted. Nor that he died."

"I could have talked him out of it. I talked him out of so many dangerous things he wanted to do."

She laughed a little and then tapped his hand. "I know you did. You were my responsible kiddo. But…" She paused, a little out of breath.

Concern for her overrode his desire to hear what she had to say. He slowed the car. "Are you sure you're up for this trip?"

"I am absolutely sure. Keep driving." She waited until he'd sped back up. "Nate, your father and I wanted to talk both of you out of enlisting, but that seemed selfish. You boys felt called to serve your country. How could we interfere with that?"

A mule deer stopped nibbling a green plant to stare at them as they drove by.

But Nate didn't quite buy it. "I feel like Tom enlisted for other reasons than to serve," he said.

"I'm sure he did, like a lot of other young men," Mom said, surprising Nate. "But the upshot was, he served. He gave his life for his country. I hate so much that it happened, but I'm proud of him. Proud of you, too."

"I wish…" Nate trailed off.

"You wish you could have saved him from himself, but you couldn't. He was always a risk-taker. I'm sure he requested the riskiest assignments on purpose. That's who he was."

"And I wasn't." Nate had gotten into some dangerous situations in his position protecting chaplains. He remembered rushing a priest to a dying man's side while shooting flared around them and an army jeep burned close by. Remembered covering a rabbi with his body when a bomb blast had surprised them on a trip they'd expected to be routine.

But those kinds of occasions were the exception. He'd also had the opportunity to spend a lot of time reading. And he'd gotten some great mentoring from a couple of the men he'd protected. "I got so many benefits from the military, way more than I expected. Whereas Tom—"

"We can't know what God had in mind," she said quietly. "We never do. But He's in control, Nate, so you don't have to be."

He knew that was true. He just hadn't applied it to his own situation. A weight seemed to lift off his shoulders.

He grasped her hand, squeezed it. "Thanks, Mom."

"You're welcome to my motherly wisdom anytime you want it. Even sometimes when you don't."

He felt a sudden urgency to learn everything he could from Mom, who was indeed wise. There was no telling how much time she'd be with them.

"Look, there's A Great Yarn, the one with the red-and-pink sign."

He pulled in and then walked into the store with her, thinking more about what she'd said. He guessed it had been self-absorbed of him to think he could have stopped Tom, or that he even should have. It was true, Tom had died the death of a hero, serving his country. Maybe Nate needed to focus on that.

Maybe he didn't have to beat himself up quite so much for Tom's death.

The yarn store was a completely alien world, full of women: several sitting around a table knitting, others browsing, a couple of workers talking to them with loud animation. One greeted his mother fondly and they went immediately toward a rack of pastel yarn. Not knowing what else to do, Nate trailed along.

"I'm in the market for a *lot* of baby yarn," Mom said, her voice cheerful. "I'm going to be laid up for a while, and I need something to do."

"We can help with that," the woman said, putting an arm around Mom and giving her shoulders a gentle squeeze. Obviously, she knew Mom's health wasn't the best.

After they'd selected what seemed like a huge amount of yarn and his mother had purchased it, spending an amount of money that made Nate wince, the clerk offered to ball the yarn, whatever that meant. "Just have a seat, and we'll be done in half an hour," the woman said.

As soon as they were settled, Nate turned to her. "Why are you going to be laid up?"

The corners of her mouth turned down. "I didn't mean for you to hear that. But since you did…well. There's a new drug regimen I'm going to be starting, and apparently there are some side effects. Extreme fatigue is one of them."

"Do you have to?" Mom was already weak.

"It's the only option, and your father and I agreed I need to give this a try."

His heart ached for her, and for Dad, and for himself. For all of the family. "I'll be with you every step of the way," he said.

"You're a good son." She looked around the

yarn store. "I want to be able to make your sister a baby afghan. I've made them for all the kids, and she just let me know—" Mom clapped a hand over her mouth. "I probably wasn't supposed to tell you. Gina is expecting again."

"That's great news." He looked toward the counter at the stack of yarn the clerk was processing. "That'll make a big baby blanket."

She smiled, her eyes a little watery. "I plan to make a couple for your kids, too. And there's no time like the present to get started."

Nate's heart stuttered. Beneath her words was a clear message: she might not be there by the time he had kids.

He wanted to argue with her, but he knew from his experience doing pastoral counseling that being overly positive could be painful to seriously ill people. So he just swallowed hard. "Thank you. I'll treasure them." His throat closed up.

She put an arm around him. "We know we'll all be together again one day."

"I know." And he'd said those words to numerous people who were grieving, or worried about, a loss. They helped, but they didn't take away the sadness. When his mother passed away, Nate was going to miss her terribly.

"Until then," Mom went on, "don't forget that life is short. Don't spend your time—waste your time—blaming yourself for something that was never really under your control."

"I'll try," he croaked.

"And seize love while you can," she said. "I cherish every minute I've had with your father and with you kids."

Nate wanted to be that way, too. To cherish the moments.

To *have* the moments, moments and, hopefully, years of love with a family of his own.

Before that could happen, though, he had something to set right. Before he could move forward with Hayley, he needed to talk to Stan and explain the new, real reason why he had to reveal the truth about Jeremy's parentage.

So he could try to move ahead in his relationship with Hayley.

That was what he wanted. It was clearer and clearer to him. He'd meet with Stan tomorrow, or this weekend at the latest. He'd *make* Stan see his point of view.

Nate watched his mother make her way over to the table of women to chat, saw her greet everyone, ask about people's kids and grandkids and jobs. The women exclaimed over her and made a place for her to sit down, and soon she was smiling and talking with them.

Nate hadn't even known she had friends in Fallsville, but one thing he'd learned about his mother: she made friends everywhere she went. It was because she was always concerned about others and rarely spent time thinking or worrying about her own problems.

Mom was an amazing person. The world would be worse off when she was gone, whenever that might be. He closed his eyes and prayed her new treatment would be successful, would give them more time together.

Meanwhile, he'd take her wisdom to heart, because she was right: life was too short to waste it on regrets.

Chapter Thirteen

Hayley had asked Nate to do their evening meetup in the school office, now serving as a camp office. Now she waited, trembling, for him to arrive.

She'd been on pins and needles since considering the wild possibility that Jeremy could be her biological son. It seemed ridiculous that he would be here, now, the needle in the haystack. But maybe it was a God thing.

Twenty times in the hours since this afternoon, when Jeremy had talked about being born in this area, she'd walked into the office determined to check his birth date. But she had never had the courage to open his file.

Partly, it was because she wanted so much for it to be true. Partly, she was terrified that it *was* true.

And the person she wanted beside her when she learned the truth was Nate.

That thought gave her pause. She'd gotten so close with him, had come to trust him. He was a wise man, even though he wasn't much older than she was. He had the spiritual depth from his training, but he also had courage from his time in the war, and sympathy from all he'd gone through, losing his brother and facing his mother's serious illness.

Oh, he was everything she wanted in a man. Wants that were newly minted because she'd never allowed herself to want a relationship before. She didn't deserve it. Except…maybe she'd been wrong about that.

The weight of the guilt she'd carried for all this time had become too heavy to bear and she was now starting to think that maybe, just maybe, it was misplaced. Maybe she'd been foolish and self-absorbed all this time to focus on her own sins and failings. After all, one of the biggest tenets of the Christian faith was that nobody deserved good things, but through Christ, God gave them out anyway.

Maybe she *didn't* have to be alone. Maybe she had something to give a husband and a family.

Maybe Jeremy is my son.

If it were true… The very thought took her breath away.

It didn't mean she would try to change anything about his life. Wherever her son was, he'd settled in with his family and she had no right to try to make any changes.

But if it was true…if it was Jeremy…

She reached for the computer. Why not access the files right now?

Except that she didn't want to get her hopes dashed alone.

"Hey! Sorry I'm late." Nate came in at a fast pace and plopped down into a chair.

"Busy day?"

He nodded. "I ended up spending a few hours with Mom after my shift."

"Everything okay?"

"Fine." He must not want to talk about his mom, because he was studying her attentively. "You look nice."

"I do?" She glanced down at her plain red T-shirt and denim shorts.

"You look nice every day," he said. "I just don't always tell you." His voice was soft and warm.

Heat rose to her face. Outside her office, she could hear the cafeteria assistants banging pans as they finished up for the evening. The lingering smell of the pasta with meat sauce they'd had for dinner permeated the air. She gripped the smooth wooden edge of her chair.

Her goal tonight was to find out the truth and deal with it, and she wanted Nate to be there. She needed his support.

But she put her quest on pause for another minute so she could just look at him. His dark, attentive eyes seemed to draw her, to reveal the soul beneath the surface. His broad shoulders denoted reliability and strength.

And he hadn't stopped looking into her eyes. Flustered, she turned back to the computer. "I... I have to look something up," she said.

"That's fine. I have this week's paperwork to finish up." He went to the file cabinet and pulled out a sheath of forms.

Hayley took a deep breath and then clicked on Jeremy's file.

There, near the top, was his birth date.

She gasped and collapsed back against the chair. The room seemed to spin around her. As if from a distance, she heard Nate's concerned voice.

"Hayley! Are you okay? What's wrong?"

She couldn't answer.

Jeremy was her son.

Her *son*.

Just this afternoon, they'd baked cookies and groomed Snowflake together. Now it turned out that she'd been hanging with her biological son.

Her heart was so full that her feelings seemed ready to detonate, filling the air with fireworks.

This could only be God's doing. God, who'd pulled apart two souls and then brought them back together. Gratitude filled her, and love for her child.

Maybe it wasn't her right to feel that. Maybe a stronger person would just set the love aside, because her son was with the mother who'd raised him, just where he should be.

But she'd loved her baby from the moment she'd held him. She'd thought about him every day since.

And now she knew almost for certain that Jeremy was the child she'd been thinking of and praying for. Jeremy was her son.

He was such a good kid, so smart, kind, good with other kids and even with dogs. He was tall—tall like his biological father, but with a slightly darker version of her own hair color, her own grey eyes.

But he was anxious, a tense kid. Was that her fault, for placing him for adoption?

"You're scaring me. Hayley, what's wrong?" Nate's words, coming from above her, his warm hands on her shoulders, brought her back to the here and now.

She was too moved to speak. Instead, she pointed at the computer screen and he leaned over her shoulder to see.

"What's that, Jeremy's admission file?"

She turned to face him, slowly. Reached up

and gripped his hand. "You know how I told you I had a baby and placed him for adoption?"

He nodded.

"Jeremy was born on the same day my son was born."

"Same year?"

She nodded slowly. "Nate, I think he's my son." Even saying the words was terrifying. She searched his face, waiting for him to tell her she must be delusional.

The surprise she'd expected didn't appear on his face. "Ah, Hayley. I wish…"

Why wasn't he surprised? But she couldn't think about that. Her mind was racing with her discovery. "I don't understand why he showed up at the camp the very year I started working here. Is it a God thing? He said he was curious about his biological mom. Could Arlene know?"

Nate's expression was…something strange. Almost resigned. Almost as if…

Her heart was pounding impossibly hard. "I just can't believe it! I mean, of course it's possible there could be two boys born on that day and placed for adoption." She flipped through the electronic file. "Could his birth certificate be here? Some of the boys use that for ID, but others use a passport or some other form of ID. And since he's adopted… No, no birth certificate. Man." She searched the application form. "I

wonder if there's any other way to tell? I mean…"
She was breathing hard, almost panicking. "Isn't
this amazing?"

Nate wasn't saying anything and, all of a sudden, his silence seemed loud.

When she looked at him, his expression was
peculiar. Set. Again, resigned.

A huge contrast to her own shock and emotion. Why?

A horrible suspicion grew in her. "You're not
surprised."

Slowly, he shook his head back and forth.

"You knew."

He drew in a breath and let it out slowly, his
eyes never leaving hers. "I was informed in a
confidential setting—"

"You *knew*." She stood quickly, paced the office, her breathing rapid. "How could you know
and not tell me? We worked with Jeremy together. You saw us getting closer. Why didn't
you tell me?"

"Confidentiality is part of my job," he said.

"So if you knew…then it's true? For sure?"

He looked at her for a long moment and then
nodded.

She flopped back in her chair, limp as a rag
doll. So it was true. The child she'd borne in
such pain and suffering had become a part of
her daily life.

Unbeknownst to her, and yet known to Nate.

She thought of them sitting together with Jeremy, hanging out with him. Thought of brushing Snowflake with him. "Jeremy doesn't know."

Nate shook his head. "I don't believe so."

She stared at Nate and thought of the time they'd spent together. Talking over everything. Sharing stories from their past. Planning and playacting their pretend relationship, which had started to feel real.

Trusting him. *Kissing* him.

And all that time, he'd known something life-changing and hadn't told her. He must have been hiding it every single time they were together. Her anger about that was a lot more clear-cut than the soup of emotions around Jeremy.

"You knew, and didn't tell me. How can I ever trust you again?"

Hayley couldn't relax. Even though it was after eleven and she had to be up early, she paced her cabin restlessly.

What was she to do with the information she'd discovered, information Nate, the jerk, had confirmed?

How had he learned about it? Did Arlene know, and had she told him? But why would she have? She didn't go to Nate's church. And, supposedly, the adoption was to remain closed forever. The agency had had a few facts on file about Hayley, mostly medical information, but Hayley had never received any information about the adoptive family.

Now that she knew, how was she to act around Jeremy, who—her heart twisted painfully—was starting to question his situation and to want information about his birth parents?

Her longing to see him, to talk to him and to hug him was as powerful as the pain she'd felt when she'd placed him for adoption. It was as if this new information had opened up a floodgate of worries and settled them all on Jeremy, this young boy she'd just gotten to know.

If she found a way to tell him the truth, if Arlene would even allow that, would that be the best thing for him? Or too much of a shock?

She picked up her Bible and flipped it open then put it down. She was too agitated to read anything, even God's words. Too agitated to think.

She would normally have turned to Nate with a moral question like that. But Nate had known all along and had withheld the information. How could she ever trust him again? As her pastor, her friend, her potential boyfriend?

She wasn't sure what to do about Jeremy, but she did know what to do about Nate: stay as far away from him as possible for as long as possible.

* * *

On Sunday evening, Nate tried hard to make the outdoor worship service the best it could be.

Nature had cooperated with warm, clear weather. The sky was darkening, and every time he looked heavenward, he saw more stars. Within an hour, they would coat the sky as if someone had spilled diamonds there.

The boys were used to the weekly routine now, and most sat quietly. But Nate's heart wasn't in performing the service. His message was basic, probably too basic even for a group of young teens. Even so, he stumbled over his words. His reading of the New Testament passage was lackluster.

Fortunately, Reggie led the boys in some praise songs that were catchy enough to get the majority of the boys involved.

When Snowflake started to howl along, everyone broke out laughing, and afterward, they all clustered around Jeremy and the panting white dog.

Nate joined in, wanting to check on Jeremy's state of mind. Ever since the terrible discussion with Hayley on Friday, when she'd learned the identity of the son she'd placed for adoption, he'd been worried that Jeremy would somehow find out the truth in a way that hurt him.

Of course, Hayley was a good person and was not likely to blurt anything out to Jeremy. She wasn't selfish and she'd figure out the best way to do it. Nonetheless, he wanted to check for himself.

Jeremy was talking and laughing, animated. One thing was for sure: camp was good for him. He looked worlds different from the anxious boy who'd arrived at Bright Tomorrows Camp just a few weeks ago.

Reassured about that problem, Nate decided he needed to go knock on Hayley's door.

He'd spent a lot of time praying about the situation, and he'd sent her text messages and tried calling, too, but she was ignoring him. Every nonanswer flattened him and that, more than anything, told him that he cared about her, a lot, and that he had to make this up. Had to fix it.

His heart rate accelerated as he approached her front door, and sweat dripped down his back even in the cool evening air. He could hear music playing inside.

He knocked then rang the doorbell. Saw her peek out through the door's high glass.

But she didn't come out. The volume of the music increased.

After five minutes, he realized she wasn't going to come out.

He sucked in a breath, let it out in a sigh and trudged away.

He was halfway to the parking area when he

saw Stan, walking. The older man usually moved fast, but after his health troubles, he was walking more tentatively. It was easy for Nate to catch up, but first, he had to dispel the surge of anger that rose in him.

Because of Stan, his relationship with Hayley was ruined. His chance of being with this woman he'd come to care for so much…gone. Just gone.

He approached Stan from behind and greeted him. "It's good to see you out and about," he said, going automatically into pastor mode.

The older man looked at him sharply. "I'm fine, but how are you?"

"Okay. Why?"

"You don't seem okay. Your sermon was off."

Nate's eyes narrowed. Great. The man who'd caused all his problems was now judging him.

The moment he had that thought, he scolded himself. Stan had revealed something important and he'd needed to do it. That was what a pastor was for.

"So what is it, Nate?"

He looked over at the man, whose sharp blue eyes seemed to pin him. Then he glanced around to make sure they had their privacy. In the distance, the boys' laughter was audible. The golden remains of the sunset revealed no one else on the dirt road except the two of them.

He'd intended to talk to Stan about this anyway. No time like the present. "Hayley found out that Jeremy's her son," he said.

Stan stopped walking. "What? How?"

"She was talking to Jeremy, and he said a few things…like where he was born. She got curious and looked up his birthday."

Stan's eyes narrowed. "There could have been a lot of boys born in Colorado on that day and placed for adoption."

"She knows, Stan. When she told me, my reaction was not what she expected, and she realized that I already knew."

They continued walking, slowly. Stan let out a sigh. "I suppose it was bound to happen," he said. "With them being together all the time. Just make sure you don't tell Arlene."

Nate frowned. "I don't think it's a secret that should remain a secret," he said. "At the very least, the adults involved should discuss it."

"Hayley and Arlene?" Stan frowned. "I can't imagine that would go well."

"Maybe not," Nate said, "but the longer it's hidden, the more possibilities of problems."

"I don't want to be involved. Arlene will kill me if she learns I knew something and didn't tell her."

"Yeah," Nate said. "Hayley is pretty mad at me, too."

"Because you knew?"

"And didn't tell her." He sighed. "I was going to come to you again to see if I could convince you to be okay with my revealing it to her. Since you told me in confidence. But before I could do that, she found out and learned that I know. Now she's not speaking to me."

Stan clapped a hand on Nate's back. "Women. They get so emotional."

"Yeah. And so do men." They reached the parking lot and Nate turned toward his truck, then turned back. "Are you going to be okay getting back to your cabin?"

"Yeah. I need the exercise." He put a hand to his heart. "I hope you can make it up to Hayley," he said. "Being old and single isn't a good thing."

"But you have Arlene—"

Stan shook his head. "We haven't made a commitment. Anything could happen."

As the older man turned and started back toward his cabin, Nate couldn't help noticing his slumped shoulders and the slow pace of his walk.

Stan was vital, strong, but he'd been felled by illness. Just as Nate's mother had been.

You never knew what was coming, and life was short. But if he compared his mother's situation with Stan's, it was Mom who'd done it right.

She'd spent a lifetime caring for others and building a family, and now, in her hour of need, they were all there for her.

Stan, whether through personal issues or bad timing, had never married. He didn't have kids, and while he dated, there was no one here for him for the long term.

Which did he want to be? It was obvious. Nate wanted to be more like his mom. Wanted to build a family around himself.

Unfortunately, he'd managed to nix his one possibility of that.

Moreover, he'd done it because of his own efforts to be perfect. To be the perfect pastor who didn't break a confidence. To be a perfect camp director who worked closely with his co-director.

He wanted to be perfect because his brother hadn't had that option, because Nate was basically living for two.

But by trying to do that, he had messed everything up. The conflict had been impossible, with no solution.

With God all things are possible.

As soon as he thought of that one line of scripture, multiple more came to him. He often counseled people who couldn't see any options ahead, and he almost always saw more than they could see themselves.

It wasn't that he was such a brilliant guy. It was the wisdom of scripture.

Casting all your care upon him; for he careth for you.

In the world ye shall have tribulation: but be of good cheer; I have overcome the world.

He got into his truck, but rather than go straight home, he pulled off on a scenic overlook. He sat in his truck and watched the sun set over the mountains. The highest peaks still had snow on them, in patches, and the sun turned them to rose-gold. A few clouds mingled to the west, making the color even more gorgeous.

"What are You looking for here, Lord?" he asked. "I want to be a good person, and I'm failing miserably."

No direct answer—Nate didn't tend to get those—but he did feel an answering warmth.

Why callest thou me good? There is none good but one, that is, God.

If Jesus had said that even he wasn't good, then what business did Nate have with trying to be so good all the time?

Nate knew that the Lord was trying to tell him something by filling his mind with verses, but for now, he couldn't see what solution there was, if any. Instead, he simply felt a growing sense of peace.

Not that he wouldn't have to do something, work hard to try to fix things with Hayley. Not that he didn't have to give the solution to God.

It was all going to work out, or it wasn't, and only God knew which.

Chapter Fourteen

On Monday afternoon, Hayley was in the Bright Tomorrows cafeteria kitchen, chopping onions and crying.

After the shocking revelation that Jeremy was her biological son, and that Nate had known it all along, she had fallen apart.

She'd sent an SOS text to Ashley and Emily on Saturday, but they'd both been away for the weekend. They'd both called and knew the basic outline of what had happened. They'd expressed all the sympathy and love in the world, and it helped, but Hayley still hurt.

Jeremy was her *son*. She'd given that precious boy away right after he was born. In her head, she knew it had been for the best, and that she had done the only thing she could do at the time.

Her heart was wrecked, though. She had given him out into the unknown. She'd given up the chance to love him, feed him, watch him take his first steps. She'd made it so he'd be placed with a mom like Arlene, who wasn't a bad person but didn't seem to be warm and easy either.

Now, Hayley had had the chance to get to know and like him as an individual, to spend time with him and get a little close to him. That was wonderful and terrible at the same time.

Nate had known all about it and hadn't told her.

What did that say about their relationship?

The thoughts had circled in her head all weekend, and she'd cried so much that she'd stayed away from church. Even if she'd been able to get it together to get dressed and attend, she doubted she could sit and listen to Nate sermonizing without calling him out. He talked a good game. But when it came to real-life events, not so much.

She'd worked her weekend shifts but had managed to stay in the background. The counselors must have thought she was sick; they'd stepped up and taken on more responsibility.

But that couldn't continue. Work didn't stop just because her world had fallen apart. Kids still needed to be fed, and that was Hayley's job.

"Hey, girl!" Ashley came through the door to the cafeteria, Emily close behind. "How are you doing?"

"She's crying." Emily hurried to stand beside Hayley, putting an arm around her.

Hayley cleared her throat and gestured with her knife toward the pile of onions. "That's why I'm crying."

"Uh-huh." It was obvious that Emily wasn't convinced. "We're worried about you."

"I didn't think you'd be back until tomorrow." Hayley rinsed her knife and covered the onions with a glass bowl. "Man, those are strong."

"What else needs chopped?" Ashley asked.

Hayley pointed to the stack of tomatoes and peppers. "Those, if you feel like helping. I can mix up the dough while you chop."

Soon her two friends were chopping vegetables while Hayley assembled the rest of the ingredients for their Tex-Mex lasagna. Being with her friends was comforting. At least a little.

"So, explain again what happened," Ashley ordered. "You found out Jeremy is from Colorado and was adopted."

"Yeah, and all of a sudden I looked at him and realized we had the same coloring. Blond hair, grey eyes. And he was the right age. Didn't want to get his hopes up, so I looked up his birthday in our materials and…" She paused to collect herself. "It's the day I gave birth."

"Oh, wow." Emily came over and hugged her from behind. "Do you feel sure he's your baby?"

"Yes," she said. "Because of Nate."

"He confirmed it? How did he know?"

"Some congregation member must have told him about it, although I don't know how anyone would know. It was a mostly closed adoption." She bent to grab some baking pans and slammed them onto the counter. "Who knows? The thing is, he didn't tell *me*."

"That stinks." Ashley finished seeding and chopping the peppers. "Where do you want these?"

"Pop them in this pan. So, yeah, he was a jerk and I'm mad at him," she said, stirring. "Most of all, though, I'm heartbroken. I would never have guessed Jeremy was my biological child." Her throat tightened and it was hard to get more words out. "He's such a great kid. I can't believe I placed him for adoption."

"Hey," Ashley said. "You did the best you could at the time. Making an adoption plan can be the kindest and best thing you can do for a baby, even though it has to hurt."

"It broke my heart. Still does."

The two of them sat and talked with Hayley for another hour. They helped her prep food for the next day, as well, lightening her load. Their presence and reassurance, and lack of judgment, was a comfort. They were good friends.

Suddenly, Nate burst through the door of the

kitchen, his shirtsleeves rolled up haphazardly, his hair on end, as if he'd been raking his fingers through it. "Have you seen Jeremy?"

"No." Hayley quelled the rush of contradictory emotions that rose at the sight of him. "Why, what's wrong?"

"What's wrong is that he's missing."

Hayley's stomach dropped. Nate was talking to the others, his mouth saying words, but all she could process was that Jeremy—her son—was in danger.

For the briefest of seconds, Nate's eyes locked with Hayley's, and it was like he could feel everything she was feeling. The worry she'd have about any camper, and the additional trauma of the missing boy being her unacknowledged biological son.

Nate wanted nothing more than to pull Hayley into his arms and comfort her pain and worry away. But there was no time. "We were gathering outside for the flag ceremony," he explained quickly. "We did a head count, and Jeremy wasn't there, so a couple of the boys and Reggie went back to the residence hall. He's not there, and none of his friends know where he is."

Mickey came into the kitchen holding Snowflake's leash. The dog trotted beside him, but she was looking back and forth, sniffing the ground, panting anxiously.

"It's my fault," the boy said in a choked voice. "I wanted to play with Snowflake, and I dared Jeremy to try to make it until dinner without her. He said he could, and he came over to the dining hall early, and now he's gone."

Hayley's face went white and she looked at Ashley and Emily.

"He came in early?" Ashley asked.

"Do you think he heard us talking?"

About what?

"I saw him running out earlier," Mickey explained. "I thought maybe he forgot something at the dorm. Either that, or he was a wreck without his dog. I went looking for him a little later, because I started feeling bad, but I couldn't find him. It's my fault he ran away!"

Nate put a hand on Mickey's shoulder. "No use assigning blame. Let's put that energy into searching."

"Do the rest of the boys know he's missing?" Ashley looked concerned.

Booker stepped forward. "The boys on our hall do. They're all looking for him."

"I'll go organize them into two or three groups," Ashley said. "That's what we did when Landon went missing. We'll fan out from here, where he was last seen." She put an arm around

Hayley and gave her a hug. "Don't worry. We found Landon and we'll find Jeremy."

But Hayley looked more upset than ever, and Nate knew why. Landon had started a fire that had nearly destroyed one of the cabins. He'd been close to being hurt or killed himself.

"You stay with us," Nate said to Booker and Mickey. "You're Jeremy's closest friends. Where does he go when he needs to get away?"

Booker frowned. "There's a trail that goes over to the ranch next door. He likes to take Snowflake over there to see the horses."

"Mickey, you and I will go there," Emily said, "and we'll take Snowflake along. Maybe Snowflake can find him. Booker, you come, too."

Nate nodded. "Good. Nobody should search alone. Hayley." He looked at her and realized she was shaking and nearly frozen. Even though she was furious with him, he knew he could help her stay calm, as calm as was possible. "We'll do the insides of buildings. Starting with this one. There are all kinds of places to hide."

"Yes. Okay." She looked almost blank with panic.

They searched methodically; the kitchen, the cafeteria and then the classrooms. Most were locked, including the shop classroom where the boys had spent time. They didn't talk, beyond sharing quick instructions and reports.

Where could the boy have gone? Nate knew he'd be found quickly—he couldn't have gone far—but there was no sign, and no phone call from the others to indicate success.

They went outside and down to the dormitory, and checked everywhere they could think of, including the run-down shed where the Margolis boys had been caught smoking before.

Hayley was like a wounded deer. She was searching, hard, but she was so shaken Nate wondered whether she could even think.

Finally, he texted Ashley and Emily, and learned that neither had found anything. Ashley and her squads were still searching, but Emily returned with Mickey, Booker and Snowflake. She shook her head. "We didn't find him."

Emily put her hands on her hips. "I don't know Snowflake and her routines enough to know how to get her to help," she said. "Should we call Jeremy's mom?"

Nate and Hayley locked eyes again. He knew they were both thinking about the volatile woman and her likely reaction.

Overhead, dark clouds were gathering. It looked like they were in for a late-afternoon storm.

Hayley glanced upward and then straightened her shoulders. "She might know how to direct Snowflake. I think we should call her."

"If we call," Nate said, "she'll get hysterical."

"We need Stan," they both said at the same time.

Because in so many ways, they thought alike. Too bad Nate had ruined the possibility of a real lasting connection between them.

"I'll run and get Mr. Stan," Mickey said. "I know where his cabin is."

Meanwhile, the rest of them searched nearby areas, but to no avail, and soon Stan was coming toward them at a too rapid pace. Nate rushed to meet him, followed by Hayley.

Mickey had already explained the situation. Stan, who appeared to have taken it in calmly, now called Arlene.

After he'd gotten out a couple of sentences, they all heard her reaction. Screaming.

Hayley looked gray. She was having a mother's reaction, too.

Stan said calming things and got a conversation going with Arlene. Minutes later, he ended the phone call. "She says to be playful with Snowflake. Say 'Where's Jeremy?' Give her something of Jeremy's to smell. It's a game they play sometimes."

"I'll get one of his socks so Snowflake can smell it." Mickey ran toward the residence hall.

Emily turned to Nate, Stan and Hayley.

"Mickey said Jeremy doesn't much like going into the woods, especially by himself."

Lightning flashed overhead, followed by a boom of thunder. Nate's stomach sank at the thought of the timid boy out in the storm.

Mickey ran back out with a whole handful of dirty socks. He thrust them at Snowflake. She wagged her tail. A few of the campers and a couple of counselors who'd been searching with Ashley milled around, watching.

"Where's Jeremy?" Hayley asked.

"Where is he, girl?" Emily chimed in.

She yapped and looked at them expectantly. "Go," Emily said. "Go find him."

The dog just sat.

"Maybe we should get Lady to help," Emily said doubtfully.

"Let's a few of us walk with Snowflake," Nate said. "We'll take the road, since Mickey says Jeremy doesn't like the woods. Stan, you stay at the school building in case Jeremy comes back."

Drops of cold rain hit them as they searched along the road. Snowflake seemed to get into the spirit of it, running and sniffing. Emily's husband, Dev, brought Lady, and the shaggy service dog lent a new energy to the search.

They divided into two groups and took opposite sides of the road, each group with a dog.

Forty-five minutes later, they had combed the

entire area on either side of the school road, to no avail. Rain was falling steadily now, thunder and lightning crashing overhead.

Hayley was shivering, and Nate was cold himself, but there was no going back. If they were cold, how was Jeremy managing alone?

A big car came toward them, headlights on, driving too fast. "Idiot," Dev muttered.

The car screeched to a halt and Arlene got out of the passenger side. A man who wore workman's clothes exited the drivers' seat and came around to hold an umbrella over Arlene.

"Have you found him?" Arlene asked, her voice near hysteria.

"Not yet," Nate said.

She glared at him then at Hayley. "I blame the two of you."

Chapter Fifteen

Arlene's words stabbed at Hayley with the sharp blade of truth. This *was* her fault. She'd been talking with her friends about being Jeremy's mom, and he must have come in and heard her. Evidently, it wasn't good news to him because he'd run away.

Snowflake trotted up to Arlene and sat before her, seeming to cower. Maybe Hayley was ascribing human feelings to a dog, but Snowflake's ears and tail drooped as if she were ashamed.

Arlene knelt and reached for the dog. "Why didn't you stick with Jeremy, girl?"

The Samoyed lifted her nose and howled.

"It was *my* fault!" Mickey's voice sounded choked. "I made Jeremy give me Snowflake to play with!"

"Then you should be ashamed of yourself,"

Arlene snapped. "Jeremy needs his dog. No telling where he is, and all alone."

"Hey now." Stan, who'd just joined them on the road, glared at Arlene. His voice sounded like that of the disapproving schoolteacher he so often was. "Blaming a child won't help."

"Her son is missing, Stan," Hayley said. "She can't be expected to be calm." She turned to Arlene. "How can we get Snowflake to help us search for him?"

"The…the game," Arlene said, her voice tight. "How do you do it?"

Arlene straightened, clapped once and then slumped again. "Jeremy loves the game," she choked out between sobs.

In the midst of her worry, Hayley felt glad to see that Arlene could be warm and emotional. Obviously, she cared deeply for Jeremy. That made up for the abrasive parts of her personality in Hayley's book.

"Can you show us how to play it?" she asked gently.

Arlene stood straight, throwing back her shoulders and sucking in a deep breath. She clapped her hands. "Want to play, do you, girl? Let's find Jeremy! Where's Jeremy? Go get him!"

Snowflake barked once and then took off like a shot, headed for the main road rather than the school. The sun emerged from behind the clouds, revealing drips of water flying up as the dog's big paws hit the puddles on the dirt road.

"We need to follow her," Hayley said.

"But what if…" Nate trailed off.

"Any better ideas?"

"Yes," Nate said. "Some of us need to follow Snowflake, but the boys shouldn't all be leaving camp at once. We could end up with more kids missing."

Quickly, he gathered the counselors and campers who'd been helping with the search and, after a short huddle, they seemed to come up with a plan. Reggie took a group of boys back up the road and another counselor took the other half down a maintenance road.

Hayley, Nate, Arlene and Stan followed Snowflake, hurrying to keep the fluffy white dog in sight. At a bend in the road, the dog gave two sharp barks. Minutes later, they heard a boy's shout.

"Snowflake!"

"Is that—"

"It's Jeremy!"

They all started running, and sure enough, there in the distance, a boy knelt by an ecstatic Snowflake at the side of the road.

Relief washed over Hayley, intense and sweet.

"Jeremy! Get off the road!" Nate's voice was stern and deep and apparently caught Jeremy's attention. The boy moved farther onto the berm, looked at them and then shouted, "Mom!"

Hayley's heart almost stopped. Her son was calling for her.

But of course, he wasn't. He was calling for Arlene, who rushed to him. The two embraced at the side of the road, with Snowflake jumping and bounding around them. Stan, Hayley and Nate hurried up to them.

A truck whooshed by and then a car.

"We need to get off the main road," Nate said. "Come on, everyone. You can talk while we head back up to the school. I'll text the others to let them know Jeremy has been found."

They all headed for the long dirt driveway that led to the school. Arlene had her arm tightly around Jeremy, and Snowflake walked on the boy's other side. The dog seemed to smile with pride.

They were almost halfway up the drive when Jeremy pulled away from Arlene and pointed at Hayley. "Is she really my birth mom?"

Time seemed to stand still.

"What?" Arlene's voice was sharp, shrill. "No, of course not!"

Stan put a hand on her shoulder. "Actually... do you remember the research you had me do?"

She spun on him. "You said you didn't find any answers."

"I didn't want you to know but…" He nodded sideways at Jeremy, as if to remind Arlene of his presence.

Arlene straightened her back and looked directly at Hayley. "Did you have a baby?"

She swallowed. "Yes. Something Jeremy said made me double-check his birth date. It's the same date I gave birth to the baby boy I then placed for adoption."

Stan and Nate walked a little away, giving the three of them privacy. But, thankfully, staying near enough to intervene if anyone—especially Arlene, who was red-faced and shaking—lost it.

Hayley focused on Jeremy. "I was poor and an addict, running with the wrong crowd. I knew I couldn't take care of you well. Placing you for adoption was the hardest thing I ever did."

He knelt down beside Snowflake and wrapped his arms around the dog's neck.

"I've thought about you every day since then." She glanced at Arlene and then knelt so that she was at Jeremy's same level. "I think I did the right thing, even though it was so hard. I can see how much you love your mom, and how much she loves you."

Arlene sank to her knees, as well, seeming oblivious to the mud and dirt defacing her elegant trousers. "I don't know what to say."

Hayley gave her a watery smile and then looked back at Jeremy. "I hope we can talk more about it once we're all warm and dry and have had some time to think. But it's all up to your mom."

Arlene pressed her lips together.

Nate came over and reached one hand out to Jeremy, the other to Hayley. "Seems like a good time to go back to camp. You missed lunch, but I'm pretty sure there are leftovers."

Stan was helping Arlene to her feet.

As Jeremy walked ahead with Nate, Arlene turned on Hayley. "You haven't handled this revelation professionally," she said. "I'll have something to say about that when I speak with the rest of the board."

Hayley sucked in a breath of mountain air, rich with spicy sage, and blew it out in a sigh. The sun peeked through clouds, casting a golden light on its way behind the mountain. A magpie scolded from the fence beside the road. She wrapped her arms around herself, still cold.

"That's understandable," she said through chattering teeth. "As long as Jeremy is safe, nothing else matters."

Her own efforts to control events and do the right thing had gone way off the rails. Now, it was all in God's hands.

The next morning, Hayley felt like she'd been hit by a truck.

Jeremy had refused to go home with Arlene as

she'd asked, insisting he wanted to stay at camp with his new friends.

"How can I let you stay at a camp that lets campers get lost?" Arlene's face had been red, as if she'd been about to cry or shout, at Jeremy, or maybe at everyone.

"I didn't get lost, Mom. I ran away. They can't watch over us all the time."

His calm reasonableness filled Hayley with amazement and love for her child. Apparently, it had convinced Arlene, too, because she'd reluctantly let him stay at camp.

Late last night, Hayley had emailed Arlene to ask for permission to talk to Jeremy about his adoption. Arlene's return note had started out with angry criticism but ended with reluctant permission for Hayley to talk to Jeremy, if he felt up to it.

So, after breakfast, she took the boy aside and shared some ugly truths about herself. No graphic details, but a further explanation of why she'd decided to make an adoption plan for him.

He sat beside her on the bench that overlooked the staff cottages and ball field. He listened to her story and asked a few questions. Mostly, he kept sneaking glances at her face, as if trying to process the idea that she was his mother.

"I loved you too much to try to raise you," she said.

"You're not an addict now," he pointed out, sounding skeptical. "You're in charge of the camp."

"You know what made the difference and helped me change?"

He shook his head.

"I found God," she said. "In fact, it started to happen in the halfway house, with the people who helped me manage my pregnancy and your adoption. They were so kind, and so full of faith. I wanted what they had. It took a while, but I read the Bible a lot and started going to church, and eventually, I dedicated my life to Christ." She studied Jeremy's face. Was that too abstract for him? Did he believe her?

"I knew God all along," he said matter-of-factly.

She started to put an arm around him and then stopped herself, unsure of what level of physical affection was appropriate between them. "That's just one reason why it's so good you were adopted. I'm glad you grew up in a family of faith. Your mom gave you a wonderful gift."

He nodded. "Mom's high-strung, but she loves me."

The confidence in his voice made Hayley both heartbroken and happy. She swallowed hard. *This* was what she'd wanted for her child: for him to know he was loved. By his family and by God.

He gestured toward the playing field below them. "I gotta go play baseball."

"Go, have fun," she said. "We can talk anytime, as long as it's okay with your mom."

She watched him go, her heart warm and aching. It was all so much. So much more, and so much less, than she wanted.

As he jogged toward the baseball field, Nate came up beside him and they walked together, talking with animation.

Nate.

He'd lied to her by omission, and she was furious at him for that. But he'd been someone to lean on yesterday when the world had seemed to fall apart. Her feelings about him swirled like a kaleidoscope.

He'd texted her this morning, offering to take over director duties for the whole day.

She'd texted back. Thanks.

She was furious at him and yet she needed his help and kindness. She watched as the two reached the rest of the boys and merged into the group.

Hayley didn't know how long she stood there, staring at the group of boys and at the mountain. Finally, she shook herself out of the fog of emotion and turned back toward the Bright Tomorrows building. She was glad to have a day off from overseeing the camp, but there was always more paperwork to do, more meals to plan and prep.

As she approached the school, a colorful vehicle caught her eye. It was a VW, with the top down and two people inside. They must be tourists. She walked forward to redirect them.

The car pulled up to the side of the road and she recognized the man and woman inside it. Her heart skipped a beat then started pounding hard.

"Mom? Dad?"

Chapter Sixteen

What could she do but smile at her parents, hug them awkwardly and bring them into the cafeteria for an early lunch?

As she led the way, as they all made polite chitchat, Hayley kept stealing glances at them. Her father wore wire-rimmed glasses now, and his hair was gray, but it was still long and pulled back in a ponytail. Her mother's hair had a few strands of gray, too, and she wore it loose and flowing around her shoulders. Both looked healthy, slender, youthful. As befitted a couple of fiftysomethings who'd had few responsibilities their entire lives.

Bitterness warred with a childish desire to please them. "Sit down, and I'll bring out some coffee and snacks."

"We're vegetarians," her mother called after her.

Of course they were. They were sensitive to the plight of farm animals.

Too bad they hadn't been sensitive to the needs of their own child.

She brought out tea and coffeecake and plunked all of it down in front of them. "How did you find me? Or...you *are* here to see me, right?"

Her mother's smile wobbled. "Of course we're here to see you, honey," she said in a husky voice. "We need to talk to you."

"Okay." That must mean something was wrong. Or maybe they needed something. Money? She schooled her face into neutrality. In her lap, her fists clenched and unclenched.

"We're getting older," her father said, "and... well, we've been feeling some guilt."

That, she hadn't expected to hear. They couldn't mean what she thought they meant. Could they?

"Guilt about what?"

"About you."

Finally! She lifted her chin and studied them like she would have studied a camper apologizing for misbehavior. Were they sincere? Could guilt make up for egregious neglect of duty?

A good Christian should instantly smile and forgive. But Hayley had longed for their love for way too many years, had written letters begging them to come and get her, or at least come and *see* her. She'd watched her grandmother scrimp and save to get her extra birthday gifts in an effort to make up for her parents forgetting to send

anything. Almost worse were the times they'd
sent something totally inappropriate: a jolly, tod-
dler-style princess card when she'd turned fifteen, a tie-dyed shirt in colors she'd never liked
and wouldn't wear.

Though she *had* worn it to bed every night
for months.

She looked at their clothes now. Expensive,
perfectly fitted, on-trend hippie clothes in flat-
tering colors. Big surprise.

Her father was speaking again. "Leaving you
with your grandmother was the hardest thing we
ever did, but we just weren't equipped to raise
a child."

Chills ran up and down Hayley's back. She'd
just said almost the exact same thing to Jeremy.

"Leaving you with your grandmother was
best," her mother said. "Or at least, we thought
so. Were we right?"

Hayley thought of the woman who'd set aside
her own retirement plans to raise a difficult grand-
daughter. Slowly, she nodded. "She was great. To
me and for me. I don't know if I was good for her,
but yeah, she was great." Her eyes filled with un-
expected tears. "I wish she were here."

Her mother let her head drop into her hands.

"That was our biggest mistake," her father
said. "Not coming to you when she passed away."

"We didn't know until after the funeral was

over," her mother said. "We should have come then."

Hayley bit her lip. "The truth is, I didn't know until after the funeral either. I was occupied with other things." Like figuring out how to manage an unplanned pregnancy and deciding what path to take after that.

Her mother gripped her hand, briefly, and then let it go when Hayley flinched.

"We have no excuse," her father said. "We were terrible parents."

Hayley couldn't disagree.

The door to the cafeteria opened and a group of boys came in. Ready for lunch. A minute later, another group arrived, the baseball players, including Jeremy and Nate.

What kind of a parent had Hayley been to Jeremy? Talk about neglect!

If her parents' mistakes were bad, her own were worse.

And when she compared Nate's faults to her own and to those of her parents, his sank into the realm of "not worth getting mad about." Or certainly, at least, forgivable.

No one deserves forgiveness, but God gives it anyway.

She looked at her parents. "Nobody's perfect," she said. "I understand that better than you think."

"Thank you," her mother said. A tear rolled down her cheek.

Now it was Hayley's turn to pat her mother's hand. She pointed to Jeremy, who was rough-housing with another boy while Snowflake sat, eyes bright, ears upright. "See the kid in the red shirt?"

They both nodded.

"I got pregnant with him when I was seventeen. That's why I didn't know until later that Grandma had died. She'd kicked me out."

"He's our grandson?" her father said, staring at Jeremy.

"I placed him for adoption," Hayley said. "I only met him again this summer."

Her parents looked at each other and then at Jeremy. Her mother put a hand over her mouth. Her father's eyes were shiny.

Around them, the noise of an active group of boys rang out: shouting and horseplay. Happiness.

"He's your grandson," Hayley said slowly, working it out as she spoke, "but you can't meet him now. He's dealing with finding out that I'm his biological mom. We can't add more to his plate."

"Hey!" Jeremy ran over to her and stopped abruptly, a few feet away. "Sorry. I didn't see you were talking to somebody."

"It's okay," Hayley said, and introduced her

parents by their first names. "How was batting practice?"

"I hit the ball three times," he said proudly. He stretched his shoulders back and forth.

Hayley glanced at her mother, who glanced back. That was a gesture her father always made.

Both she and her mother teared up.

"C'mon, Jeremy!" another boy called.

He started to run off then turned. "Nice to meet you," he said.

Her father gave a wave. Her mother smiled.

Neither of them seemed to be able to speak, and Hayley wasn't either.

She just pressed her hand to her chest and wished Nate were there beside her.

Saturday was the community open house. Nate wasn't sweating it; it was to be casual, informal, a way to build connections between Bright Tomorrows and the surrounding area. He hoped it would be fun.

The boys all wore their yellow Bright Tomorrows shirts, while the counselors' shirts, and his own, were dark blue with yellow lettering. Clusters of campers worked at various stations. One group had set up three tents and built a campfire, demonstrating their outdoor skills. Another group was doing something with paint at a couple of picnic tables pulled together. Yet another group was gearing up for a tug-of-war. A few of the oldest campers had been designated tour guides and were leading people around the grounds, explaining what they were seeing.

The smell of grilling burgers and hot dogs made Nate's mouth water, and the sound of a small kazoo band made him smile. Reggie had dreamed up kazoo-playing as a rainy-day activity, and the boys who'd taken to it were actually pretty good.

He would have loved to share his enjoyment with Hayley, but that wasn't going to happen. She didn't seem furious anymore, but neither was she the friendly, warm companion he'd come to care for more and more. She was calm, but distant, and seemed to have a lot on her mind. Probably some of it being related to the fact that her parents had come to see her after many years away. And then, of course, there was Jeremy.

He'd tried to talk to her about all of it, but she'd politely dismissed his efforts.

The romance between them was gone. He'd lost his chance.

"Mr. Nate, the popcorn machine isn't working!" Booker was beckoning frantically.

Since they'd borrowed the machine from Nate's church, he knew its idiosyncrasies and was able to quickly fix it.

They had a good turnout, which wasn't surprising. The people of Little Mesa embraced the Bright Tomorrows school and camp and seemed glad for the chance to show support. The boys did skits, including one that involved Jeremy and Snowflake, and it was a huge hit. Stan and Arlene were there, and they clapped as hard as anyone.

So, that was good. Arlene was getting over what she'd seen and learned. Nate didn't know if she and Hayley had talked or not.

Because Hayley wasn't sharing anything with him.

When there was a lull, he approached Hayley. He hated that she looked guarded. "Just FYI," he said, "I'm going to tell my mom the truth about us. That we're not really dating."

"Good," she said fervently. "Hiding the truth is never a good idea."

"Hayley, I'd love to talk to you about—"

She held up a hand. "I don't want to get into it, okay?"

"Do you want to be there to talk to my mom?"

"Maybe for a little bit." Her guard slipped. "I'm near the edge, to tell you the truth. It's been quite a week."

"Then don't come, it's okay."

"No, I will." She nodded toward the parking lot. "Actually, I think your mom is here now."

"What?" He turned and saw his mother in her wheelchair, with Dad pushing it. She looked pale, which made sense. She hadn't been feeling well and he was surprised that she'd come.

He speed-walked over to her. "Are you sure you're up to this?"

"No, I'm not sure," she said, her voice cross. "But I get tired of being stuck at home. I need to get out and see life and people."

"Of course." He took her hand and walked beside her. He was a little surprised that she was cranky, but only because it was Mom, who was always positive.

Even she was allowed to have a down day, though.

Across the field, he saw Jeremy and Snowflake. They'd stopped beside Hayley, while Arlene looked on with a frown. Hayley seemed to notice because she said something to Jeremy, smiled and turned away.

That was Hayley. Always looking out for others. She didn't want Arlene to get upset.

On impulse, Nate waved to Jeremy and beckoned him over. "Jeremy, this is my mom, Mrs. Fisher. Can she meet Snowflake?"

"Sure!" Jeremy smiled at Mom. "You can pet her if you want."

Mom's face broke into a happy expression. "She's a beauty." She rubbed a hand over Snowflake's head and ears. The dog seemed to sense that she needed cheering up and stood patiently for petting, all the while panting up at her with her trademark smile.

"She knows some tricks," Jeremy said. "Want to see?"

"I sure do," Mom said.

Jeremy snapped his fingers to get Snowflake's attention, and gave a command. Snowflake sat up on her haunches, front paws in the air, and caught a treat Jeremy tossed to her.

Mom clapped delightedly.

A sudden idea came to Nate. Would Mom like an ESA? Or, at any rate, a pet?

While his mother continued to chat with Jeremy and admire Snowflake's tricks, Nate walked over to where Arlene stood surveying the scene with a critical air.

"Question for you," he said. "Does Snowflake have any siblings?"

She frowned over at him. "I would think a camp director would have more to do than chat about pets."

So she was in *that* mood. It made sense, given how recently she'd learned about Hayley. Her whole view of Jeremy and his presence at the camp must have undergone a radical change.

He gestured toward his mother and Jeremy. "My mom's really enjoying Snowflake, and it occurred to me that she might benefit from an emotional support dog."

"And why would *that* be?"

Nate blew out a breath. "She's...well, she's pretty sick." His throat closed and he had to stop talking.

Arlene glanced at his face, looked over at his mother and Jeremy, and then, awkwardly, patted him on the back. "That must be hard for you," she said. "I can give you the name of the organization where we got Snowflake. They're wonderful."

"Thanks," Nate managed to say.

"Swim races are starting," someone yelled.

Nate had agreed to serve as a judge, so he headed down to the pool to do his duty. Then he got caught up in organizing a tug-of-war between campers and counselors.

An hour later, during a lull in activities, he approached Hayley. She'd been talking to a couple of the boys, and they must have said something funny, because she threw back her head and laughed.

He loved that about her; that she was honest with her emotions and always ready to laugh. Not to mention how beautiful she looked, her hair golden in the sun, her cheeks flushed. His heart pounded, being close to her. If only things had worked between them.

She looked over at him and raised an eyebrow, her smile disappearing.

"I'm going to talk to Mom about us now, before she gets tired and has to leave," he said. "You said you wanted to be there?"

"Sure." She walked beside him in the direction of the picnic table where Mom was sitting with Dad. "Can we sit for a minute?" he asked his parents.

"Always room for our favorite couple," Dad said heartily.

"We might not be your favorite for long," Hayley said, and looked over at Nate.

He cleared his throat and dove in. "We've been deceiving you about being a couple," he said. "The truth is, we're just friends." As soon as he said that, he looked at Hayley. *Were* they still friends? And could his own feelings really be described as just friendly?

Hayley reached out and took his mother's hand. "I'm so sorry. We wanted to make you happy, so when you assumed we were a couple, we just went with it. That turned into basically lying about our relationship, which was wrong. I just want you to know that I…" She swallowed. "That I love your family and I'm sorry." She got up, gave a little wave and hurried away, her eyes wet with tears.

They all watched her go and then Mom and Dad looked at each other. "Should we tell him?" Dad asked.

"I think so. You see," she said, turning to face Nate, "we've known all along."

"What?" He stared at his mother then at his father.

"We knew you weren't a couple," Dad said.

"From the beginning?"

Mom nodded. "It was just wishful thinking on my part, and I knew it. But then the two of you jumped in to say you actually *were* a couple. I hoped that playacting love would lead to the real thing, because you're perfect for each other."

Nate's head was spinning. "We might have *been* perfect for each other, but I ruined it." He looked up at the mountains surrounding them, his heart full of regret.

"Don't you think," Mom said, "that with God all things are possible?"

Nate blew out a breath and looked from Mom to Dad. "I *should* believe that, but I'm struggling. She's not angry with me anymore, but she's avoiding me, which is almost worse."

"You need to find the right way to spend time with her," Dad pronounced. "Somewhere she can't get away and hide."

Mom looked at Dad, and her face broke out in a huge smile. "I have a great idea," she said.

Chapter Seventeen

⌐◞

On Monday after lunch, Hayley was cleaning up the cafeteria when Jeremy burst in. "Will you come down to the waterfall with me and Snowflake?"

Hayley's heart seemed to expand and warm and ache all at the same time. Dozens of times each day, she experienced a little shock, realizing that Jeremy was her son, and she was able to see him and talk to him and share with him a little of the love she'd always held in her heart.

She'd stayed in touch with Arlene by email, and the woman was slowly warming up to the idea of making Jeremy's adoption open, since it had basically already happened.

Arlene and Stan had spent time together at the open house. She seemed to have forgiven Stan for his role in the deception. Just as Nate's mom had instantly forgiven Nate and Hayley for deceiving her.

Their examples, plus a lot of prayer, had led Hayley to mostly forgive Nate for keeping the truth about Jeremy's identity secret from her.

Now, though, she wasn't sure where they stood.

They'd been cordial, if cool, to each other during the week since the truth had come out. They'd worked together efficiently.

But the spark they'd shared had gone way underground. Maybe it had been entirely extinguished, from Nate's side at least.

"Will you come?" Jeremy was still looking at her hopefully.

"Of course." She put away her rag and took off her apron. "I'd be glad to walk down there with you, as long as you let someone know where you're going."

"I did."

"You're sure? We can run over and see your counselor now—"

"No! I told him, and Mr. Nate, too." Jeremy's forehead wrinkled, like he was afraid she didn't want to be with him. It was a feeling Hayley remembered from her own childhood all too well. Being rejected by a parent was a horrible thing.

When, in fact, she treasured every minute she could spend with her amazing son, getting to know him better. "Then let's go!"

Soon they were hiking down a wide, well-used path toward the waterfall. The sky was a spotless blue and a magpie scolded from the branch of a piñon pine. Snowflake trotted alongside, plunging into the bushes a couple of times. Jeremy didn't stop her.

"You realize she's going to need brushing after this," Hayley said.

"That's okay. You can help me." Jeremy smiled at her tentatively. "Want to?"

"We'll see." Hayley was thrilled he wanted to spend more time with her, but she also had to remember that he wasn't truly her child. He was Arlene's. Arlene had watched him take his first steps, and gotten him ready for kindergarten, and encouraged him to learn his manners and be kind to others. "Maybe your mom will want to come up and help you."

He shrugged and nodded. "Probably, she will."

Hayley felt bittersweet happiness, seeing that Jeremy was so confident in his adoptive mother's love.

They threw a stick for Snowflake and stuck their hands into the freezing waterfall. Jeremy used a stick to dig in the sand and shouted over the sound of the water, talking about how he wanted to go back and dig for dinosaur bones soon.

Hayley treasured every second, but all too

soon, her duties called. "Come on, kiddo. I need to go back."

He looked at his watch. "Not yet. Free time isn't over."

Even though she adored being with him, she was the adult, and she couldn't let him run the show. "I need to get some things done."

Finally, he agreed, and they hiked back up the hill and through the trees to the school.

And she gasped.

There, in front of the school, was a partially inflated hot-air balloon, a rainbow of bright red, yellow and blue zigzags.

And there was Nate, standing in front of it, beckoning to her.

She pressed her hands to her face as she walked to him. "What's this all about?"

"Happy birthday two days early," he said. He gestured to the crowd of boys on the school's porch.

"Happy birthday, Miss Hayley," they yelled, and broke into an off-key chorus of "Happy Birthday" accompanied by Reggie's guitar and the kazoo band.

She laughed, and clapped, and thanked them, hugging those who didn't mind it.

Normally, she didn't like a fuss for her birthday. She hadn't planned to tell anyone.

But…what a great treat.

"You thought of this?" she asked Nate amid the boys' talk and noise and the poofs of gas and flame the pilot was using to inflate the balloon.

"I did, with a little help from my mom. She's amazing at doing online research to find out birthdays."

"Thank you. And please thank her for me."

"Time to climb aboard," the pilot called to them.

Nate held out his arm.

She took it and walked with him, overwhelmed.

At the basket, the pilot's helper pointed out the footholds and gestured for someone to bring a step stool. "It's like getting on a horse," she said as she helped Hayley, then Nick, climb in.

There was a quick safety briefing that Hayley had trouble hearing over the noise of the gas bursts. Above them, the balloon was huge, far bigger than she'd expected when seeing balloons in the air.

And then the balloon lifted off, as gently as a soap bubble blown from a child's wand, to the sound of the boys' cheers. The heat from the balloon burners had them shedding their jackets.

It was utterly silent, and beautiful. No wind, because they were a part of the wind, floating on the currents.

Nate stood close as they looked out over the

mountains and pointed to landmarks, familiar and unfamiliar.

Inside, beneath her excitement, her heart was practically screaming. Why? Was all of this really for her birthday?

She looked over at Nate, taking in his strong jawline and broad shoulders, his relaxed stance as he leaned on the lip of the basket. Finally, she asked him.

"What made you think of this?"

He smiled at her. "I felt like I needed to apologize for deceiving you, in a big way. And I've heard you say how much you like hot-air balloons."

"I've always loved them," she said. "This was so sweet." And not cheap.

And maybe, not something a "just friends" friend would do.

Her nerves sparked and she skittered away from that thought. "Look," she said, "the church! And you can see the cars on Main Street, like little toys."

He leaned close to look, and she could smell his cologne, could see the slight stubble on his face. He glanced down at her. They were so close. She couldn't stop herself from glancing at his lips, and then she looked away, her face heating.

"I want to talk to you about something." His voice was serious.

Her heart started thumping and fear washed over her.

"I've known you so long, and we've been friends. And I screwed up."

She tried to laugh. "Yeah, you did."

"I'm so sorry, Hayley. I made a big mistake, not finding a way to be open with you. I hurt you and I apologize for that. With all my heart."

"I've already forgiven you." Reading the doubt in his eyes, she squeezed his hand. "Somebody wise once told me that everyone makes mistakes. I guess that's even true for a pastor."

He laughed a little. "It is." His eyes crinkled. "You know how we've faked having a relationship?"

She nodded.

"I want to make it real."

Her heart rate jumped a few more levels. The giant balloon above them, the pilot's discreet presence, the trees and rivers rushing by below... all of it seemed to fall away and there was only Nate's face, his serious eyes.

"What are you talking about when you say you want to make it real?" Sudden insecurity washed over her and she was once again the little girl whose parents claimed to love her but didn't show it in their actions.

He studied her then brushed a hand over her hair. "Things can change in a moment, and life is short." He reached into his pocket, pulled something out and sank to his knees. "Hayley, when I say I want to make it real, what I mean is…will you marry me?"

Nate's head was spinning, and not from the gentle motion of the balloon. It was from his own actions.

What on earth was he doing on his knees?

The floor was hard plywood, its edges bound in leather just as the borders of the basket were. When he looked up, he saw controlled gas flames and the riot of glowing colors that made up the balloon.

But most of all, he saw Hayley's stunned face.

He'd intended to ask her to try dating him. Maybe, if he sensed she was on board, to suggest an exclusive relationship.

He'd had no intention of pulling out the ring in his pocket. Or at least, not much of one. It was way too soon.

When that lost, sad expression had flashed over her face, though, he'd skipped right over the preliminaries. He'd sensed, maybe wrongly, that she needed the reassurance of knowing the whole scope of his feelings.

But did that mean he had to jump the gun and propose marriage?

He got to his feet and put a hand on her shoulder. "Listen, I'm sorry. That was way too rushed."

She looked shell-shocked.

The balloon floated along, heat from the burners making his already hot face hotter. He looked down at the fields below, trying to find his grounding. But it wasn't there, of course. He let his eyes close for just a moment. Every ounce of the poise he used to lead a congregation, every bit of courage he'd summoned while serving overseas, seemed to have deserted him.

I'm messing this up, Lord. Help!

Since Hayley still hadn't said anything, he blundered on. "I just... I have the ring. It's my mom's engagement ring. She wants me to give it to the woman I marry." He held the open box out to her.

Hayley looked at it, eyes wide. "Doesn't she want to wear her ring?"

"It doesn't fit her anymore." His throat tightened on the words as he pictured Mom's thin hands.

Hayley put her hand to her heart, her mouth twisting. "Oh no. I'm sorry."

"Don't be. It made her so happy to give it to me. To us." He swallowed hard. "But I get it, it's way too soon. I should just be grateful you'd go on this ride with me and let me apologize."

"Of course," she said faintly.

"Hayley, meeting you was the best day of my life. And becoming your friend has made these past couple of years happy, in spite of everything my family's been going through."

"I'm glad." Her head tilted and she studied him as she leaned back against the edge of the basket. That was Hayley. She always seemed to *see* him.

Behind her, the scenic mountains flew by, and with them, the time for their ride. He needed to speak his piece.

"I'm a mess," he confessed. "I've been trying to avoid having any happiness my brother couldn't have. But I've realized that's the wrong focus. I want to make you happy, because you deserve it. *That's* what will make me happy."

She made a protesting sound.

"Your smile, and your laugh, and the way we talk together, and how we manage things. Just guessing here, but I think that if we can manage a camp full of at-risk boys together, we'd be great at making a family."

Her eyes widened and she sucked in an audible breath.

He was digging himself in deeper. In addition to proposing, he was talking about starting a family. What was wrong with him?

Yet inside, he knew he wanted to spend the rest of his life with this woman. Wanted to father children with her, to raise a family together.

He'd spent so much time praying this past week and God had given him peace about it.

He'd just jumped the gun a little on the timing. Okay, a lot. A woman like Haley needed to be romanced slowly. She was truly worth it. She deserved it.

"I'm in love with you, Hayley. But don't worry. I'm not really proposing."

She blinked and shook her head, rapidly, and then started to laugh. "Are you asking me to marry you or aren't you?"

She was smiling big now, and that made him smile, too. She wasn't the type to hold it against him, the fact that he was incredibly awkward at this. "I would be asking, except it's too soon."

She took his hand. "Nate. Let me talk a minute."

"Of course." He blew out a breath and lifted his warm cheeks to feel the breeze.

"I really care for you, too," she said. "I always have."

His heart stuttered. Was this the beginning of a yes or the beginning of a no?

"In the past, I didn't think I deserved love. But now I'm starting to hope that maybe I do."

"You do. So much."

Their gazes locked.

He had to know. "Will you try a relationship with me?"

She shook her head. "No way."

His heart sank.

"Why would I just *try* a relationship when what I want is to marry you?"

"You want to…" Joy washed over him. "You don't have to…" He stared at her.

She held up a hand. "As long as you're singing my praises, let me sing yours, okay? I love your strength, and your gentleness, and the way you listen. I love watching you with the boys, your patience and your sense of fun. You treat me well." She shrugged. "We're good together, really good. What more could I want?"

What more could *he* want? He leaned forward and kissed her.

Epilogue

One Year Later

"We made it through another summer!" Hayley raised her hands over her head like a cheerleader and then looked around at the assembled guests. "Thank you all so much for what you've done for the Bright Tomorrows camp."

It was the end-of-summer staff celebration, with a few additional guests as well.

Ashley stood beside her. "I'm happy to announce that ten of the boys from this year's camp have put in applications to attend high school here. Combined with the eight from last year, we're on track with our enrolment goals."

A cheer went up and Hayley hugged Ashley. Between the military readiness program that Ashley and Jason had developed, and the success of the summer camps, the academy was thriv-

ing. They could all continue their work helping
boys who needed a hand up.

It made Hayley happy that Booker, who'd
learned to love Colorado, would be attending
the academy again this year.

Jeremy would attend for his sophomore year,
too, as a day student.

"Eat up, everyone!" Hayley said, gesturing toward the picnic tables laden with food. Although
she was certified as a teacher now, and would
work here in that capacity come fall, she still
loved feeding people. She'd prepared most of the
food for this end-of-summer gathering outside
the Bright Tomorrows cafeteria.

"I've got to check on the baby," Ashley said,
and hurried over to Jason, who was holding little Miranda. At the same table were Emily and
Dev and their four kids—Landon and the three
siblings they'd adopted.

Hayley surveyed the group to make sure everyone seemed happy and settled. Jeremy was
tugging Arlene toward the table next to Emily
and Dev and their kids, where Stan already sat.
Stan had recovered fully from his heart attack
but had decided to take things easy this summer
rather than coming back to directing the camp
full-time. Now that he and Arlene were married, and he was helping her to raise Jeremy, his
life was full. He was great with Jeremy and was

a calming force for Arlene, from what Hayley could see.

She was still amazed and grateful that she could be part of Jeremy's life, could see him regularly and watch him grow.

Snowflake was nudging at Titan, Dev's mastiff, but the big dog refused to be baited into playing; instead, he flopped down onto his side next to Dev. Snowflake gave up and went over to Lady, Emily's poodle mix. Emily smiled and let Lady out of the harness, and the two dogs began to chase each other around and around the happy group.

In the parking lot, a colorful VW pulled up next to the other cars, and Hayley's mom and dad got out.

Hayley walked over to greet them. Their relationship wasn't perfect, but her parents were trying, motivated largely by the opportunity to spend time around their grandson. Her father, especially, looked hungrily around until he spotted Jeremy, and then he nudged Hayley's mother and pointed. Jeremy waved to them and then went back to an intent conversation he was having with Emily and Dev's oldest foster son.

Mom and Dad would never have a real grandparenting relationship with Jeremy; it wasn't their right, any more than Hayley could become his full-time mother. But they saw him occasionally and sent him gifts from their travels. Although they did more for Jeremy than they'd ever done for Hayley, she'd released her anger toward them with Nate's help.

Nate. Her husband, the man of her dreams.

She looked around and spotted him. He was sitting at the end of one of the picnic tables with his parents, and she headed over that way. Nate's mother—her mother-in-law, whom she now called Mom—looked flushed and happy. The new treatment had sent her into remission, and although she still used a wheelchair sometimes and had to pace herself, she was an integral part of the family. Hopefully, that would be the case for a few years to come, at least.

As Hayley approached, Nate stood and came to greet her, hugging her and then taking her hand to lead her over to the table. "Come on. Mom says she has a gift for us."

Hayley lifted her eyebrows. "What's the occasion? She already got me a bunch of stuff for my birthday." Indeed, Nate's family seemed intent on showering Hayley with gifts and love, letting her know that she was fully accepted and loved.

Hayley adored them all.

Nate's mother gestured to his father, who pulled out a big brightly wrapped package from under the table. "This is for the two of you," he said. "At least, partly."

"You open it," Nate said, his arm around her.

She kissed her mother-in-law's cheek and then ripped open the package. Nestled in tissue paper was a gorgeous knitted blanket, its mix of pastels suggesting its purpose.

She looked quickly at Nate. "It's a baby blanket," she said, confused. "Did you—"

He lifted his hands, palms out. "I didn't tell them, I promise."

His mother reached out and took Hayley's hand. "I could tell from your glow," she said. "I always know. And I'm absolutely thrilled that you two are expecting."

"Oh, Mom." Tears rose to her eyes and she hugged her mother-in-law and then her father-in-law. "We're thrilled, too." She admired the beautiful blanket, folded it carefully and put it in the box for safekeeping, and then went back to Nate, who wrapped his arms around her. "Are you upset they found out?"

She shook her head. "I could never be upset about that," she said. "And now that the first trimester's safely passed, I guess we can start spreading the news."

"I feel like shouting it from the mountaintops," he said. "I'm the happiest I've ever been, married to you. But I have a feeling our baby will complete the circle."

"Only one?"

"We've talked about that. As many as you want."

Hayley's very soul felt full. She had a wonderful man, a wonderful family, friends, work, and a baby on the way.

"God is so good," she whispered. "So much more than we deserve."

"That's God for you," he said.

She kissed Nate's cheek and sent up a heartfelt prayer of thanks.

* * * * *

If you enjoyed this K-9 Companions book by Lee Tobin McClain, be sure to pick up her previous contributions to the miniseries:
Her Easter Prayer *and*
The Veteran's Holiday Home.

And look for a K-9 Companions book by Heidi McCahan coming in August 2023 from Love Inspired!

Dear Reader,

Thank you for making one more trip to the Bright Tomorrows Academy, this time in its summer camp phase.

Nate and Hayley are two wonderful people who are stuck in the past. They're blaming themselves for mistakes they made rather than trusting in God's forgiveness. It takes a whole community—and a beautiful support dog named Snowflake—to get them to embrace a future together.

Jeremy's adoption story is close to my heart because I'm an adoptive mom. I never had the opportunity to know my daughter's birth mother, but I have thought about her many times. How difficult it must have been for her to let her precious daughter go. How she must have grieved, and how hard it still must be when our daughter's birthday comes around. Due to circumstances outside of anyone's control, it's unlikely that we will have the chance to meet. Hayley is my tribute to my wonderful daughter's first mother.

To read about the other couples in this story, check out *Her Easter Prayer* and *The Veteran's*

Holiday Home. If you'd like the recipe for the chocolate-chip cookies Hayley and Jeremy baked together, visit my website, www.leetobinmcclain. com.

Wishing you much happiness and many good books,

Lee

COMING NEXT MONTH FROM
Love Inspired

LICNM0523